THE PELICAN SHAKESPEARE

GENERAL EDITOR ALFRED HARBAGE

THE COMEDY OF ERRORS

WILLIAM SHAKESPEARE

THE COMEDY OF ERRORS

EDITED BY PAUL A. JORGENSEN

PENGUIN BOOKS

Penguin Books
625 Madison Avenue
New York, New York 10022

First published in *The Pelican Shakespeare* 1964
This revised edition first published 1972
Reprinted 1974, 1978, 1980

Library of Congress catalog card number: 79-98349

Printed in the United States of America by
Kingsport Press, Inc., Kingsport, Tennessee
Set in Monotype Ehrhardt and Linotype Times Roman

CONTENTS

PUBLISHER'S NOTE

Soon after the thirty-eight volumes forming *The Pelican Shake-speare* had been published, they were brought together in *The Complete Pelican Shakespeare*. The editorial revisions and new textual features are explained in detail in the General Editor's Preface to the one-volume edition. They have all been incorporated in the present volume. The following should be mentioned in particular:

The lines are not numbered in arbitrary units. Instead all lines are numbered which contain a word, phrase, or allusion explained in the glossarial notes. In the occasional instances where there is a long stretch of unannotated text, certain lines are numbered in italics to serve the conventional reference purpose.

The intrusive and often inaccurate place-headings inserted by early editors are omitted (as is becoming standard practise), but for the convenience of those who miss them, an indication of locale now appears as first item in the annotation of each scene.

In the interest of both elegance and utility, each speech-prefix is set in a separate line when the speaker's lines are in verse, except when these words form the second half of a pentameter line. Thus the verse form of the speech is kept visually intact, and turned-over lines are avoided. What is printed as verse and what is printed as prose has, in general, the authority of the original texts. Departures from the original texts in this regard have only the authority of editorial tradition and the judgment of the Pelican editors; and, in a few instances, are admittedly arbitrary.

SHAKESPEARE AND
HIS STAGE

William Shakespeare was christened in Holy Trinity Church, Stratford-upon-Avon, April 26, 1564. His birth is traditionally assigned to April 23. He was the eldest of four boys and two girls who survived infancy in the family of John Shakespeare, glover and trader of Henley Street, and his wife Mary Arden, daughter of a small landowner of Wilmcote. In 1568 John was elected Bailiff (equivalent to Mayor) of Stratford, having already filled the minor municipal offices. The town maintained for the sons of the burgesses a free school, taught by a university graduate and offering preparation in Latin sufficient for university entrance; its early registers are lost, but there can be little doubt that Shakespeare received the formal part of his education in this school.

On November 27, 1582, a license was issued for the marriage of William Shakespeare (aged eighteen) and Ann Hathaway (aged twenty-six), and on May 26, 1583, their child Susanna was christened in Holy Trinity Church. The inference that the marriage was forced upon the youth is natural but not inevitable; betrothal was legally binding at the time, and was sometimes regarded as conferring conjugal rights. Two additional children of the marriage, the twins Hamnet and Judith, were christened on February 2, 1585. Meanwhile the prosperity of the elder Shakespeares had declined, and William was impelled to seek a career outside Stratford.

The tradition that he spent some time as a country

teacher is old but unverifiable. Because of the absence of records his early twenties are called the "lost years," and only one thing about them is certain – that at least some of these years were spent in winning a place in the acting profession. He may have begun as a provincial trouper, but by 1592 he was established in London and prominent enough to be attacked. In a pamphlet of that year, *Groats-worth of Wit*, the ailing Robert Greene complained of the neglect which university writers like himself had suffered from actors, one of whom was daring to set up as a playwright:

. . . an vpstart Crow, beautified with our feathers, that with his *Tygers hart wrapt in a Players hyde*, supposes he is as well able to bombast out a blanke verse as the best of you: and beeing an absolute *Iohannes fac totum*, is in his owne conceit the onely Shake-scene in a countrey.

The pun on his name, and the parody of his line "O tiger's heart wrapped in a woman's hide" (*3 Henry VI*), pointed clearly to Shakespeare. Some of his admirers protested, and Henry Chettle, the editor of Greene's pamphlet, saw fit to apologize:

. . . I am as sory as if the originall fault had beene my fault, because my selfe haue seene his demeanor no lesse ciuill than he excelent in the qualitie he professes: Besides, diuers of worship haue reported his vprightnes of dealing, which argues his honesty, and his facetious grace in writting, that approoues his Art. (Prefatory epistle, *Kind-Harts Dreame*)

The plague closed the London theatres for many months in 1592–94, denying the actors their livelihood. To this period belong Shakespeare's two narrative poems, *Venus and Adonis* and *The Rape of Lucrece*, both dedicated to the Earl of Southampton. No doubt the poet was rewarded with a gift of money as usual in such cases, but he did no further dedicating and we have no reliable information on whether Southampton, or anyone else, became his regular patron. His sonnets, first mentioned in 1598 and published without his consent in 1609, are intimate without being explicitly autobiographical. They seem to commemorate the poet's friendship with an idealized youth, rivalry with a more favored poet, and love affair with a dark mistress; and his bitterness when the mistress betrays him in conjunction with the friend; but it is difficult to decide precisely what the "story" is, impossible to decide whether it is fictional or true. The true distinction of the sonnets, at least of those not purely conventional, rests in the universality of the thoughts and moods they express, and in their poignancy and beauty.

In 1594 was formed the theatrical company known until 1603 as the Lord Chamberlain's men, thereafter as the King's men. Its original membership included, besides Shakespeare, the beloved clown Will Kempe and the famous actor Richard Burbage. The company acted in various London theatres and even toured the provinces, but it is chiefly associated in our minds with the Globe Theatre built on the south bank of the Thames in 1599. Shakespeare was an actor and joint owner of this company (and its Globe) through the remainder of his creative years. His plays, written at the average rate of two a year, together with Burbage's acting won it its place of leadership among the London companies.

Individual plays began to appear in print, in editions both honest and piratical, and the publishers became increasingly aware of the value of Shakespeare's name on the title pages. As early as 1598 he was hailed as the leading English dramatist in the *Palladis Tamia* of Francis Meres:

As *Plautus* and *Seneca* are accounted the best for Comedy and Tragedy among the Latines, so *Shakespeare* among the English is the most excellent in both kinds for the stage: for Comedy, witnes his *Gentlemen of Verona*, his *Errors*, his *Loue labors lost*, his *Loue labours wonne* [at one time in print but no longer extant, at least under this title], his *Midsummers night dream*, & his *Merchant of Venice*; for Tragedy, his *Richard the 2*, *Richard the 3*, *Henry the 4*, *King Iohn*, *Titus Andronicus*, and his *Romeo and Iuliet*.

9

The note is valuable both in indicating Shakespeare's prestige and in helping us to establish a chronology. In the second half of his writing career, history plays gave place to the great tragedies; and farces and light comedies gave place to the problem plays and symbolic romances. In 1623, seven years after his death, his former fellow-actors, John Heminge and Henry Condell, cooperated with a group of London printers in bringing out his plays in collected form. The volume is generally known as the First Folio.

Shakespeare had never severed his relations with Stratford. His wife and children may sometimes have shared his London lodgings, but their home was Stratford. His son Hamnet was buried there in 1596, and his daughters Susanna and Judith were married there in 1607 and 1616 respectively. (His father, for whom he had secured a coat of arms and thus the privilege of writing himself gentleman, died in 1601, his mother in 1608.) His considerable earnings in London, as actor-sharer, part owner of the Globe, and playwright, were invested chiefly in Stratford property. In 1597 he purchased for £60 New Place, one of the two most imposing residences in the town. A number of other business transactions, as well as minor episodes in his career, have left documentary records. By 1611 he was in a position to retire, and he seems gradually to have withdrawn from theatrical activity in order to live in Stratford. In March, 1616, he made a will, leaving token bequests to Burbage, Heminge, and Condell, but the bulk of his estate to his family. The most famous feature of the will, the bequest of the second-best bed to his wife, reveals nothing about Shakespeare's marriage; the quaintness of the provision seems commonplace to those familiar with ancient testaments. Shakespeare died April 23, 1616, and was buried in the Stratford church where he had been christened. Within seven years a monument was erected to his memory on the north wall of the chancel. Its portrait bust and the Droeshout engraving on the title page of the First Folio provide the only likenesses with an established claim to authenticity. The best verbal vignette was written by his rival Ben Jonson, the more impressive for being imbedded in a context mainly critical:

. . . I loved the man, and doe honour his memory (on this side idolatry) as much as any. Hee was indeed honest, and of an open and free nature: had an excellent Phantsie, brave notions, and gentle expressions. . . . (*Timber or Discoveries*, ca. 1623–30)

*

The reader of Shakespeare's plays is aided by a general knowledge of the way in which they were staged. The King's men acquired a roofed and artificially lighted theatre only toward the close of Shakespeare's career, and then only for winter use. Nearly all his plays were designed for performance in such structures as the Globe – a three-tiered amphitheatre with a large rectangular platform extending to the center of its yard. The plays were staged by daylight, by large casts brilliantly costumed, but with only a minimum of properties, without scenery, and quite possibly without intermissions. There was a rear stage gallery for action "above," and a curtained rear recess for "discoveries" and other special effects, but by far the major portion of any play was enacted upon the projecting platform, with episode following episode in swift succession, and with shifts of time and place signaled the audience only by the momentary clearing of the stage between the episodes. Information about the identity of the characters and, when necessary, about the time and place of the action was incorporated in the dialogue. No place-headings have been inserted in the present editions; these are apt to obscure the original fluidity of structure, with the emphasis upon action and speech rather than scenic background. (Indications of place are supplied in the footnotes.) The acting, including that of the youthful apprentices to the profession who performed the parts of women, was highly skillful, with a premium placed upon grace of gesture and beauty of diction. The audiences, a cross section of the general public, commonly numbered a thousand, sometimes more than two thousand. Judged by the type of plays they applauded, these audiences were not only large but also perceptive.

THE TEXTS OF THE PLAYS

About half of Shakespeare's plays appeared in print for the first time in the folio volume of 1623. The others had been published individually, usually in quarto volumes, during his lifetime or in the six years following his death. The copy used by the printers of the quartos varied greatly in merit, sometimes representing Shakespeare's true text, sometimes only a debased version of that text. The copy used by the printers of the folio also varied in merit, but was chosen with care. Since it consisted of the best available manuscripts, or the more acceptable quartos (although frequently in editions other than the first), or of quartos corrected by reference to manuscripts, we have good or reasonably good texts of most of the thirty-seven plays.

In the present series, the plays have been newly edited from quarto or folio texts, depending, when a choice offered, upon which is now regarded by bibliographical specialists as the more authoritative. The ideal has been to reproduce the chosen texts with as few alterations as possible, beyond occasional relineation, expansion of abbreviations, and modernization of punctuation and spelling. Emendation is held to a minimum, and such material as has been added, in the way of stage directions and lines supplied by an alternative text, has been enclosed in square brackets.

None of the plays printed in Shakespeare's lifetime were divided into acts and scenes, and the inference is that the author's own manuscripts were not so divided. In the folio collection, some of the plays remained undivided, some were divided into acts, and some were divided into acts and scenes. During the eighteenth century all of the plays were divided into acts and scenes, and in the Cambridge edition of the mid-nineteenth century, from which the influential Globe text derived, this division was more or less regularized and the lines were numbered. Many useful works of reference employ the act–scene–line apparatus thus established.

Since this act–scene division is obviously convenient, but is of very dubious authority so far as Shakespeare's own structural principles are concerned, or the original manner of staging his plays, a problem is presented to modern editors. In the present series the act–scene division is retained marginally, and may be viewed as a reference aid like the line numbering. A star marks the points of division when these points have been determined by a cleared stage indicating a shift of time and place in the action of the play, or when no harm results from the editorial assumption that there is such a shift. However, at those points where the established division is clearly misleading – that is, where continuous action has been split up into separate "scenes" – the star is omitted and the distortion corrected. This mechanical expedient seemed the best means of combining utility and accuracy.

THE GENERAL EDITOR

INTRODUCTION

As the most elementally and transparently funny of Shakespeare's plays, *The Comedy of Errors* would seem to need slight introduction. Shakespeare himself wisely discarded the explanatory prologue which he found in his Latin source, Plautus' *Menaechmi* (the two Menaechmuses). He allowed the play to speak for itself, to make its incredible muddle of events its adequate explanation for being. Indeed, this play is a good beginning one for the student of Shakespeare, for ability to enjoy the madness of total bewilderment is not a tutored one; every child has it. In the chaos created by two sets of twins (not to mention some four merchants), the expert is not of much help, as painstaking plot analyses of the play have shown. In telling who is who, or where, at any one time, the expert is about as helpful and impressive a guide as a professor leading a tour through a maze of mirrors in an amusement park. One does not have much time, "in the stirring passage of the day," to speculate about the full extent of the confusion, or even to say where any two or three, of the four twins, are when they are offstage creating further embarrassments.

It is, for other reasons, a good play to begin on. Unlike Shakespeare's more mature comedies, its funniness is relatively uncomplicated by social criticism, by philosophy, or by characterization. Pure comedy of event can move more cleanly, more like a detective story, to its tidy solution. There are no lingering notes of greater problems unsolved. The value of life itself is not questioned (though the point of it all may be not too clear); all that matters is rearranging human puppets so that they can again go about their proper business. There are left over no Shylocks, no Malvolios. Indeed, there is left over nothing really to think about – except, if one wishes, the tremendously puzzling question of what so grips and amuses an audience during a play which has so little thought in it. And, again if one wishes, one can see in their most elemental form dramatic strategies that Shakespeare was to use, so skilfully that they become almost invisible, in most of his later plays, tragedies as well as comedies. It is here that the critic, if he is needed at all, can point the way toward the considerable importance of what can also be appreciated as pure fun of the most hilarious kind, but a kind of fun, perhaps, that strikes deeper into the human predicament than is at first apparent.

One could speak more confidently of the elementary nature of this comedy, and of it as a significant beginning of Shakespeare's later development in the theatre, if one knew that it is indeed an extremely early play. It would be convenient to think of it as Shakespeare's first comedy. Unfortunately, the external evidence permits of a date anywhere from the beginning of Shakespeare's career to as late as 1594, when its first recorded performance was given at the Gray's Inn Christmas Revels on December 28 before a riotous audience of learned lawyers. Of little aid in establishing the date of composition is the possibility that Shakespeare used the translation by "W. W." (?William Warner) of the *Menaechmi*. This was not published until 1595, but was entered in the Stationers' Register in 1594 and may have been available to Shakespeare considerably earlier. Warner was patronized by the Hunsdons, father and son, both of whom became patrons of Shakespeare's dramatic company; an acquaintance between Shakespeare and Warner was quite possible. But Shakespeare himself could read Plautine Latin, and he may well have gotten the strange designation of "Antipholis Sereptus," which appears inappropriately in the opening stage directions at II, i, from the Latin word "surreptus" (snatched away), used in Renaissance editions of Plautus to designate one of the twin Menaechmi.

Internal evidence suggests an earlier dating. There is the reference to Spain as having sent "whole armadoes of carracks," an allusion that would have lost some of its proud currency not long after 1588. There is also a tantalizingly specific topical allusion by Dromio of Syracuse to France as "armed and reverted, making war against her heir." This is clearly a reference to the French civil wars, which concerned England so much that Elizabeth sent over two expeditionary forces. Henry of Navarre, the "heir," had been designated such by Henry III, but he had to fight for several years to secure his full right. Even when Henry III was still alive, the Catholic League waged war against Navarre. When Henry III died on August 12, 1589, Navarre became king (Henry IV), though he did not achieve Paris until 1593. But he was technically "heir" only until 1589. It is perhaps noteworthy that another very early play, *Love's Labor's Lost*, is paired with *The Comedy of Errors* in dealing with French affairs and specifically with Henry of Navarre.

The lack of compelling characterization also suggests an early date; but this quality may just as well be artistic design as immaturity, for it permits an economical exploitation of the speed and neatness of Latin comedy. *The Comedy of Errors* is precisely the sort of play that an artistically serious young dramatist, still without too much to say about love, politics, or human nature, might design as a reaction against contemporary (and perhaps his own) dabbling in romantic comedy. A date between 1589 and 1591 would accommodate most of the essential facts that we have about the play.

Although it has been held that as sources for *The Comedy*

of Errors Shakespeare drew upon every well-known Latin (not to mention Italian) comedy of mistaken identity, one play, Plautus' *Menaechmi*, is the undisputed source for the main story. But Plautus is Roman comedy at its most cynical. Elizabethans preferred a wife rather than a prostitute as the central female character, and so the Courtesan, still present, is downgraded. The English audience preferred in general some softening of the derisive, satirical spirit that constituted comedy for the Romans. Shakespeare created the attractive figure of Luciana, thus permitting a hint of the lyrical, tender, and high-spirited love interest, alien to Latin comedy, that is to distinguish his later works. He added also the "kitchen-vestal," Luce, a greasy, obese wench of the sort that Londoners would appreciate; she anticipates Touchstone's Audrey. And he enriched Plautus' Medicus into the figure of the schoolmaster, Dr Pinch, whose baleful fate and indignities may serve to warn later pedants not to deal meticulously with so robust a comedy.

Other additions are still more significant. In Plautus the father of the twins dies of grief after the loss of one twin. Shakespeare thus is responsible for the poignant, poetic role of old Egeon, whom we see only at the beginning and ending of the play. He also gives a kind of tragic overcast to the play, the sort of uneasiness in the midst of mirth that Shakespeare could never throughout his career entirely abandon. There would always be a threatened death or disaster. *The Comedy of Errors* would be slighter without this sombre background, and the reunion at the end would be less impressive if Egeon did not meet both his long-lost sons and his wife, the Abbess. For the sadness and suffering by shipwreck and the ultimate reunion – one of the major themes of Shakespearean comedy – Shakespeare was specifically indebted in this case to the Greek romance of Apollonius of Tyre (in Gower's version or in Twine's). Therein the supposedly drowned wife of Apollonius floats to Ephesus and becomes a priestess in the Temple of Diana; she is later reunited to her husband as is Egeon to the Abbess in Shakespeare. It is the Abbess who best expresses the mingled poignancy and comedy of the play: "this sympathizèd one day's error."

An even more important alteration of the *Menaechmi* was the addition of twin servants to the twin masters. Sixteenth-century Italian and Spanish versions of Plautus had experimented with more than one pair of twins, even introducing a sister; but Shakespeare was probably indebted mainly to Plautus' most popular play, *Amphitruo*. Herein – in what becomes Shakespeare's III, i, the most hilarious scene in the play – Mercury impersonates Amphitruo's servant so as to keep master and man out of the house while Jupiter (disguised as Amphitruo) is enjoying the wife within.

Shakespeare, however, needed no inspiration for the confusing quartet other than his own insight into the comic. He knew, well before Bergson brilliantly explained it, that man laughs at any imposition of the mechanical or duplicative upon the spontaneity and variety of life. Twins are, as Bergson saw, comic because they are mechanically identical. A person who looks exactly like another travesties the first by his very being; there would otherwise be no laughter at the performance of mimics. Two sets of twins increase the ludicrous trick played on man's individual ego. Shakespeare never tired of his delighted awareness that only one of a kind can have dignity. A double marriage ceremony makes a philosophical as well as ribald commentary upon a precariously civilized institution. Four simultaneous marriages, as in *As You Like It*, are not "romantic"; the sight of four couples lined up for the ceremonious mating is inescapably farcical. Likewise *The Comedy of Errors*, by having two sets of identical twins, strips all the dignity of individuality from its participants, and even in the joyful reunion there can be no identification with any one character.

With four mistakable persons wandering in a maze, plotting rather than other dramatic skills is most needed. And perhaps the symmetry and near flawlessness of this plot make it the best work of this not contemptible kind that Shakespeare was ever to do. However, though the characterization of the play is usually not praised, it is not negligible. Shakespeare merely succeeded, for one of the rare times in his career, in not allowing any one person to outgrow his function in the story. The characters, despite their comical external likenesses, are all distinct as personalities. The two Antipholuses are remarkably dissimilar for identical twins. The Syracusian brother is melancholy, earnest, and almost tragically inclined. He speaks some of the most ardent poetry in the play and would probably, given a continued sad life, have developed into the copy of his father. The Ephesian Antipholus, on the contrary, is a prosperous, rather insensitive businessman, a respected citizen who expects his wife to behave with complete moral propriety while he himself tastes, in moderation, the pleasures of the town. He is also a realistic version of the husband with a nagging wife. His brother has no wife, and when this brother meets Luciana (who is also very different from her sister) it is with the first-love ardor of any of Shakespeare's young lovers. The two Dromios are also distinct. Both are witty, but the Syracusian has the edge; and it has been his task to cheer up his pensive master. Dromio of Ephesus, like his master, has a more prosaic nature, befitting his urban environment and the not too moral respectability of his master.

There are also other interesting persons (notably Luce, who with only a few slight lines is hugely comic), but the essence of this comedy is clearly not in character. If the critic examines closely the dialogue and stage business (remembering uneasily the singed beard and fool-cut hair of the scholarly Dr Pinch), he will find that the texture of the play is made up of incessant use of a small number of low comedy elements. There are endless quibbles (mainly by the Dromios), gross accounts of the structure of Luce, tireless jokes about the cuckold's horns and the "French disease." The dialogue is animated but not memorable; this is not a comedy of subtle or even realistic language. The stage business is equally innocent of subtlety. One is aware mainly of frantic running, angry expostulation, and a rapid shifting of confusable persons on the stage. Above all one is aware of beatings, particularly blows to the head. Why this beating should be funny it is not easy to say. But Shakespeare found it merry enough to devote by large odds the greatest part of the stage business to mere blows. Each Dromio gets rewarded for his well-meaning efforts by the bloodying of the pate by both masters. Somehow the repeated act of having one's "sconce" broken is enormously satisfying to audiences. Clowns with large, artificial heads prove this to-day, taking blows growing in intensity until the thud is resonant throughout the arena. It is not, of course, funny if the victim of a mighty blow stays down. Perhaps it is the resilience of the Dromios that reassures us, even as, on a much higher (and broader) level, Falstaff rebounds from blow after blow to his ego. The blow to the head is also a blow to the pretentious part of man, gratifying the popular audience by its universally levelling virtue. One must not, incidentally, judge the length of this comedy by its scanty 1756 lines. Picture it, rather, with full stage business, dome after dome resounding from the re-peated blows – domes that also suffer the added indignities of cuckold's horns and the ravages of the "French dis-ease." It is, then, a comedy that reassures the audience that man's head is fundamentally ridiculous, not too important in any robust view of life.

But of course dialogue and stage business are secondary in this play to what it is classically famous for: mistaken identity. Mistaken identity is in itself an additional blow to the individual ego. One is seldom pleased to find that he is constantly being taken for someone else – usually, of

course, someone much less impressive. There are, however, several kinds of mistaken identity. This play em-
ploys the lowest. The two higher forms of mistaken
identity are mistaking the true nature of another person
and mistaking one's own nature. Both lead to a re-
examination of life and involve character growth.
Exteriors are important only in so far as they lead to a
realization of one's true nature. Of these two higher
forms there are only hints in *The Comedy of Errors*. Antipholus of Syracuse asks a question that might have been
all-important in a later comedy:

> Am I in earth, in heaven, or in hell?
> Sleeping or waking? mad or well advised?
> Known unto these, and to myself disguised!

This is a remote approach to the agonizing and central
question which Angelo in *Measure for Measure* asks
himself:

> What dost thou? or what art thou, Angelo? –

a question preparing him for a totally new understanding
of his own nature. On a still higher level – and showing
that mistaken identity is fundamental to Shakespearean
tragedy as well – is Lear's question:

> Who is it that can tell me who I am?

There is no probing of personality in *The Comedy of
Errors*. No one learns more about himself or his neighbor
as a result of the errors. Confusion leads to near-madness
but does not bring about the breakdown of an ego prior to
self-knowledge; it leads rather to drawn swords and
headblows. The resolution of the play is not the serene
elevation of vision which we find in the later comedies; it
is simply a recognition of who, physically, is who.

There is still another peculiar limitation in this play of
mistaken identity. No actor within the play pulls the strings

of the human puppets. There is no Rosalind, no Prospero to make the confusion delightfully purposeful. In no other play is the ignorance of the participants more total, nor in any play is the purpose of the confusion less apparent. Perhaps Shakespeare felt that by widening the gap in awareness between audience and participants he was giving the audience a pleasant sense of superiority. This, however, does not seem to be the way it works out. The audience grows almost as baffled and impatient as the participants. But here there is no Iago upon whom to vent one's sense of outraged human dignity. The purposelessness of this confusion is perilously close to the purposelessness of uninstructed life. The comedy is thus elemental in a sense that may be more important than is true of the later comedies, which seem, in contrast, to be mere playacting. Here is a basic comedy of human ineptitude without a comforting presiding spirit. Man laughing at the plight of the pointlessly outraged characters in this play is man laughing, not too comfortably, at his own most painful apprehension about life; but this apprehension, it must be stressed, is never brought brilliantly to the surface of consciousness by great poetry. It is an apprehension that might have seized Antipholus of Syracuse, but never one of the Dromios.

One must not, after all, forget that the play does not lead immediately to conclusions about human life. Theatrically it is superb farce – as so many of the so-called high comedies basically are. It is the farce of high-spirited, youthful characters, not like Egeon beyond the resilience of youth, who fight back at an intolerable situation. It is a farce set in a scene faintly anticipating the magic of *A Midsummer Night's Dream*, for Ephesus had acquired the reputation from Menander and from St Paul (Acts xix:19) of being a place of sorcerers and magic. The whole experience becomes, indeed, almost a dream. As a play of "errors," thus set in a scene of witchery, it leads man into crazy antics, gives him suddenly a wife unknown to him,

causes people he does not know to offer him presents –
almost, as would be the case in a later play, fills the land
with music at the same time one is knocked about, bound,
or claimed as her own by a fat kitchen-wench.

The play is all of these things, perhaps, for in it Shakespeare was feeling his way toward many possibilities of
dramatic growth. He could not write simple farce without
raising questions about the meaning of farce. But he does
not ask such greater questions explicitly. In his last play,
The Tempest, Shakespeare comments with great verbal
beauty upon his craft and its strategies. *The Comedy of
Errors* exhibits the legerdemain of Shakespeare's art without attempting to explain it. The basic techniques, still un-
disguised by weightier matters, are there. They are the
more valuable in that they are not the commentary of
Shakespeare the dramatic critic but of Shakespeare the
dramatist. To understand the full range of Shakespeare's
theatrical experiments, one should no more skip *The
Comedy of Errors* than *The Tempest*.

Since the prominence of the play in the rowdy "night of
errors" at Gray's Inn in 1594, *The Comedy of Errors* has
had a lively but not illustrious stage history. Although
Macklin and Kemble have played in it, it is not a work to
attract the greatest actors; it simply has no role for major
interpretation. On the other hand, it has suffered less
radical treatment by adapters than have some of the better
plays. True, there have been operatic versions and musical
comedy versions; songs from other plays have been
introduced into it; the farcical quality of the Dromios has
been exaggerated; and, in the last decade or so, novel
settings have been used in certain productions. On the
whole, however, the central features of the play have remained unchanged in revivals through the years. At
present it is very popular in Germany and in Russia.
Because of its brevity, it is sometimes paired with some
other play. A happy inspiration prompted the Old Vic
Company in 1956–57 to perform it on the same program

with *Titus Andronicus*. Thereby two allegedly Shake-spearean "primitives" could be seen as the classically designed, durable works that they are.

University of California   PAUL A. JORGENSEN
at Los Angeles

NOTE ON THE TEXT

The Comedy of Errors was first printed in the folio of 1623 probably from the author's own draft. Except for considerable confusion of character names in the stage directions and speech-prefixes, the text is a good one. There is indication (see V, i, 9 s.d. that the folio act–division was superimposed upon the original manuscript, but this division, with a further division of the acts into scenes, is provided marginally for reference in the present edition. The following brief list of departures from the folio text is complete, except for the correction of obvious typographical errors and the normalization of speech-prefixes and of such forms as the following in the stage directions: *Antipholus Ephes.* (to *Antipholus of Ephesus*), *Antipholus Siracusia* (to *Antipholus of Syracuse*), and *S. Dromio* (to *Dromio of Syracuse*). The adopted reading in italics is followed by the folio reading in roman.

I, i, 16 *at* at any   38 *too* (om. in F)   41 (and throughout) *Epidam-num* Epidamium   42 *the* he   102 *upon* up   116 *bark* bank   123 *thee* they   151 *life* help

I, ii, s.d. *Antipholus [of Syracuse]* Antipholis Erotes   4 *arrival* a rival   30 *lose* loose   32 s.d. *Exit* Exeunt   40 *unhappy* un-happy a   66 *clock* cook   93 *God's* God   94 s.d. *Exit* Exeunt

II, i, s.d. *Antipholus [of Ephesus]* Antipholis Sereptus   11 *o'door* adore   12 *ill* thus   20 *Men* Man   *masters* master   21 *Lords* Lord   45 *two* too   61 *thousand* hundred   72 *errand* arrant   107 *alone, alone* alone, a love   112 *Wear* Where

II, ii, s.d. *Antipholus [of Syracuse]* Antipholis Errotis   79 *men* them   97 *tiring* trying   101 *no time* in no time   174 *stronger* stranger   185 *offered* free'd   193 *drone* Dromio

III, i, 89 *her* your   91 *her* your

III, ii, s.d. *Luciana* Juliana   4 *building* buildings   *ruinous* ruin-
ate   16 *attaint* attaine   21 *but* not   26 *wife* wise   46 *sister's*
sister   49 *bed* bud   *them* thee   57 *where* when   109 *and* is

IV, i, 87 *then she* then

IV, ii, 6 *Of* Oh   34 *One* On   35 *fury* fairy   45 *he's* is   48 *That*
Thus   61 *'a* I

IV, iii, 32 *ship* ships   55 *if you do* if do

V, i, 33 *God's* God   121 *death* depth   155 *whither* whether
357–62 (in F these lines follow l. 346)   404 *ne'er* are

THE COMEDY OF
ERRORS

Solinus, Duke of Ephesus
Egeon, a merchant of Syracuse
Antipholus of Ephesus } *twin brothers, and sons to Egeon and*
Antipholus of Syracuse } *Emilia, but unknown to each other*
Dromio of Ephesus } *twin brothers, and slaves*
Dromio of Syracuse } *to the two Antipholuses*
Balthazar, a merchant
Angelo, a goldsmith
A Merchant, friend to Antipholus of Syracuse
A Second Merchant, to whom Angelo is a debtor
Dr Pinch, a schoolmaster and a conjurer
Emilia, wife to Egeon, an Abbess at Ephesus
Adriana, wife to Antipholus of Ephesus
Luciana, sister to Adriana
Luce, servant to Adriana
A Courtesan
Jailer, Officers, and other Attendants

Scene : *Ephesus*]

THE COMEDY OF ERRORS

I, i

Enter the Duke of Ephesus, with the Merchant
[Egeon] of Syracuse, Jailer, and other Attendants.

EGEON

Proceed, Solinus, to procure my fall,
And by the doom of death end woes and all.

DUKE

Merchant of Syracusa, plead no more.
I am not partial to infringe our laws. 4
The enmity and discord which of late
Sprung from the rancorous outrage of your Duke
To merchants, our well-dealing countrymen,
Who, wanting guilders to redeem their lives, 8
Have sealed his rigorous statutes with their bloods,
Excludes all pity from our threat'ning looks.
For since the mortal and intestine jars 11
'Twixt thy seditious countrymen and us,
It hath in solemn synods been decreed, 13
Both by the Syracusians and ourselves,
To admit no traffic to our adverse towns: 15
Nay more, if any born at Ephesus 16
Be seen at Syracusian marts and fairs;
Again, if any Syracusian born
Come to the bay of Ephesus, he dies,

I, i In Ephesus, presumably the palace of Duke Solinus 4 *partial* inclined
8 *guilders* Dutch coins worth about 1s. 8d. apiece 11 *intestine* (usually
means 'internal'; here, perhaps, intensifies *mortal*) 13 *synods* councils
15 *adverse* opposed 16 *Ephesus* (on west coast of Asia Minor)

His goods confiscate to the Duke's dispose,
21 Unless a thousand marks be levièd,
22 To quit the penalty and to ransom him.
Thy substance, valued at the highest rate,
Cannot amount unto a hundred marks;
Therefore, by law thou art condemned to die.

EGEON
Yet this my comfort: when your words are done,
My woes end likewise with the evening sun.

DUKE
Well, Syracusian, say in brief the cause
Why thou departed'st from thy native home,
And for what cause thou cam'st to Ephesus.

EGEON
A heavier task could not have been imposed
Than I to speak my griefs unspeakable;
Yet that the world may witness that my end
34 Was wrought by nature, not by vile offense,
I'll utter what my sorrow gives me leave.
In Syracusa was I born, and wed
Unto a woman, happy but for me,
And by me too, had not our hap been bad.
With her I lived in joy: our wealth increased
By prosperous voyages I often made
41 To Epidamnum; till my factor's death,
And the great care of goods at random left,
Drew me from kind embracements of my spouse;
From whom my absence was not six months old,
Before herself (almost at fainting under
The pleasing punishment that women bear)
Had made provision for her following me,
And soon and safe arrivèd where I was.

21 *marks* (worth about 13s. 4d. apiece)   22 *quit* discharge, pay   34 *nature* natural, i.e. fatherly, love   41 *Epidamnum* i.e. Epidamnus, port on the east coast of the Adriatic ('Epidamnum' was the form used by W. W. [?William Warner] in his translation of the Latin source, 1595); *factor's* agent's

There had she not been long but she became
A joyful mother of two goodly sons;
And, which was strange, the one so like the other
As could not be distinguished but by names.
That very hour, and in the self-same inn,
A mean woman was deliverèd   54
Of such a burden male, twins both alike.
Those – for their parents were exceeding poor –
I bought, and brought up to attend my sons.
My wife, not meanly proud of two such boys,   58
Made daily motions for our home return.   59
Unwilling I agreed. Alas! too soon
We came aboard.
A league from Epidamnum had we sailed
Before the always wind-obeying deep
Gave any tragic instance of our harm.   64
But longer did we not retain much hope;
For what obscurèd light the heavens did grant
Did but convey unto our fearful minds
A doubtful warrant of immediate death;   68
Which, though myself would gladly have embraced,
Yet the incessant weepings of my wife,
Weeping before for what she saw must come,
And piteous plainings of the pretty babes,   72
That mourned for fashion, ignorant what to fear,
Forced me to seek delays for them and me.
And this it was, for other means was none:
The sailors sought for safety by our boat,
And left the ship, then sinking-ripe, to us.   77
My wife, more careful for the latter-born,   78
Had fast'ned him unto a small spare mast,
Such as seafaring men provide for storms;

54 *mean* of low birth   58 *not meanly* more than commonly   59 *motions*
plea   64 *instance* clear indication   68 *doubtful warrant* disturbing omen
72 *plainings* crying   77 *sinking-ripe* ready to sink   78 *My . . . latter-born*
(l. 124 indicates, puzzlingly, that not the 'latter-born,' but the elder, went
with the mother)

To him one of the other twins was bound,
Whilst I had been like heedful of the other.
The children thus disposed, my wife and I,
Fixing our eyes on whom our care was fixed,
Fast'ned ourselves at either end the mast,
And floating straight, obedient to the stream,
Was carried towards Corinth, as we thought.
At length the sun, gazing upon the earth,
Dispersed those vapors that offended us,
And by the benefit of his wishèd light
The seas waxed calm, and we discoverèd
92   Two ships from far, making amain to us:
93   Of Corinth that, of Epidaurus this.
But ere they came – O let me say no more!
Gather the sequel by that went before.

DUKE

Nay, forward, old man; do not break off so,
For we may pity, though not pardon thee.

EGEON

O, had the gods done so, I had not now
Worthily termed them merciless to us!
For ere the ships could meet by twice five leagues,
We were encountered by a mighty rock,
Which being violently borne upon,
103   Our helpful ship was splitted in the midst;
So that, in this unjust divorce of us,
Fortune had left to both of us alike,
What to delight in, what to sorrow for.
Her part, poor soul, seeming as burdenèd
With lesser weight, but not with lesser woe,
Was carried with more speed before the wind,
And in our sight they three were taken up
By fishermen of Corinth, as we thought.
At length another ship had seized on us,
And knowing whom it was their hap to save,

92 *amain* speed   93 *Epidaurus* town in Argolis on the Saronic Gulf   103
helpful ship i.e. the mast

Gave healthful welcome to their ship-wracked guests,
And would have reft the fishers of their prey,   115
Had not their bark been very slow of sail;
And therefore homeward did they bend their course.
Thus have you heard me severed from my bliss,
That by misfortunes was my life prolonged,
To tell sad stories of my own mishaps.

DUKE

And for the sake of them thou sorrowest for,
Do me the favor to dilate at full,   122
What have befall'n of them and thee till now.

EGEON

My youngest boy, and yet my eldest care,
At eighteen years became inquisitive
After his brother; and importuned me
That his attendant – so his case was like,   127
Reft of his brother, but retained his name –
Might bear him company in the quest of him;
Whom whilst I labored of a love to see,   130
I hazarded the loss of whom I loved.
Five summers have I spent in farthest Greece,
Roaming clean through the bounds of Asia,
And coasting homeward, came to Ephesus,
Hopeless to find, yet loath to leave unsought
Or that or any place that harbors men.   136
But here must end the story of my life;
And happy were I in my timely death,   138
Could all my travels warrant me they live.   139

DUKE

Hapless Egeon, whom the fates have marked
To bear the extremity of dire mishap!
Now trust me, were it not against our laws,
Against my crown, my oath, my dignity,

---

115 *reft* robbed   122 *dilate* relate   127–28 *attendant . . . name* (referring to the slaves, each named Dromio)   130 *of a love* out of love   136 *Or . . . or* either . . . or   138 *timely* speedy   139 *travels* (with a secondary sense of 'travails' or labors)

144   Which princes, would they, may not disannul,
        My soul should sue as advocate for thee.
146   But though thou art adjudgèd to the death,
        And passèd sentence may not be recalled
        But to our honor's great disparagement,
        Yet will I favor thee in what I can.
        Therefore, merchant, I'll limit thee this day
151   To seek thy life by beneficial help.
        Try all the friends thou hast in Ephesus ;
        Beg thou, or borrow, to make up the sum,
        And live ; if no, then thou art doomed to die.
        Jailer, take him to thy custody.

JAILER
        I will, my lord.

EGEON
        Hopeless and helpless doth Egeon wend,
        But to procrastinate his lifeless end.   *Exeunt.*

*

I, ii   *Enter Antipholus [of Syracuse], a Merchant, and
               Dromio [of Syracuse].*

MERCHANT
        Therefore give out you are of Epidamnum,
        Lest that your goods too soon be confiscate.
        This very day a Syracusian merchant
        Is apprehended for arrival here,
        And not being able to buy out his life,
        According to the statute of the town,
        Dies ere the weary sun set in the west.
        There is your money that I had to keep.

---

144 *disannul* annul   146 *the death* the sentence of death   151 *beneficial help* i.e. help by a benefactor
I, ii The mart in Ephesus   s.d. (The folios have 'Antipholis Erotes,' the 'Erotes' being probably a corruption of 'Erraticus,' the wanderer. In II, i, likewise, Antipholus of Ephesus is called 'Sereptus,' for 'Surreptus,' the lost or stolen one.)

ANTIPHOLUS S.

Go bear it to the Centaur, where we host,   9
And stay there, Dromio, till I come to thee.
Within this hour it will be dinner-time;
Till that, I'll view the manners of the town,
Peruse the traders, gaze upon the buildings,
And then return and sleep within mine inn,
For with long travel I am stiff and weary.
Get thee away.

DROMIO S.

Many a man would take you at your word,
And go indeed, having so good a mean.   18

Exit Dromio [of Syracuse].

ANTIPHOLUS S.

A trusty villain, sir, that very oft,   19
When I am dull with care and melancholy,
Lightens my humor with his merry jests.   21
What, will you walk with me about the town,
And then go to my inn and dine with me?

MERCHANT

I am invited, sir, to certain merchants,
Of whom I hope to make much benefit;
I crave your pardon. Soon at five o'clock,   26
Please you, I'll meet with you upon the mart,
And afterward consort you till bedtime.   28
My present business calls me from you now.

ANTIPHOLUS S.

Farewell till then. I will go lose myself,
And wander up and down to view the city.

MERCHANT

Sir, I commend you to your own content.   *Exit.*

9 *Centaur* (the name of an inn; houses, shops, and inns were identified, not by numbers, but by signs bearing pictures, such as that of a centaur or a phoenix) 18 *mean* means, opportunity (Dromio is a bondman) 19 *villain* servant (used good-humoredly) 21 *humor* mood (in Renaissance psychology, humor was a fluid in the body, determining disposition and temperament) 26 *Soon at five o'clock* i.e. towards evening 28 *consort* accompany

ANTIPHOLUS S.

He that commends me to mine own content,
Commends me to the thing I cannot get.
I to the world am like a drop of water
That in the ocean seeks another drop,
37   Who falling there to find his fellow forth,
38   Unseen, inquisitive, confounds himself.
So I, to find a mother and a brother,
In quest of them, unhappy, lose myself.
          Enter Dromio of Ephesus.
41   Here comes the almanac of my true date.
What now? How chance thou art returned so soon?

DROMIO E.

Returned so soon! rather approached too late.
The capon burns, the pig falls from the spit,
45   The clock hath strucken twelve upon the bell;
My mistress made it one upon my cheek:
She is so hot because the meat is cold;
The meat is cold because you come not home;
49   You come not home because you have no stomach;
You have no stomach, having broke your fast;
But we, that know what 'tis to fast and pray,
52   Are penitent for your default to-day.

ANTIPHOLUS S.

53   Stop in your wind, sir; tell me this, I pray:
Where have you left the money that I gave you?

DROMIO E.

O, sixpence, that I had o' Wednesday last
56   To pay the saddler for my mistress' crupper?
The saddler had it, sir; I kept it not.

ANTIPHOLUS S.

I am not in a sportive humor now.

---

37 *forth* out   38 *confounds himself* loses itself, mingles indistinguishably
41 *almanac ... date* i.e. in Dromio, Antipholus sees his own age   45 *twelve*
(half an hour late for the usual dinner-time)   49 *stomach* appetite   52
penitent suffering (from hunger)   53 *wind* words   56 *crupper* strap
attached to saddle and passing under horse's tail

Tell me, and dally not, where is the money?
We being strangers here, how dar'st thou trust
So great a charge from thine own custody?

DROMIO E.

I pray you, jest, sir, as you sit at dinner.
I from my mistress come to you in post;   63
If I return, I shall be post indeed,   64
For she will score your fault upon my pate.
Methinks your maw, like mine, should be your clock   66
And strike you home without a messenger.

ANTIPHOLUS S.

Come, Dromio, come, these jests are out of season;
Reserve them till a merrier hour than this.
Where is the gold I gave in charge to thee?

DROMIO E.

To me, sir? Why, you gave no gold to me.

ANTIPHOLUS S.

Come on, sir knave, have done your foolishness,
And tell me how thou hast disposed thy charge.

DROMIO E.

My charge was but to fetch you from the mart
Home to your house, the Phoenix, sir, to dinner;   75
My mistress and her sister stays for you.

ANTIPHOLUS S.

Now, as I am a Christian, answer me,
In what safe place you have bestowed my money;   78
Or I shall break that merry sconce of yours   79
That stands on tricks when I am undisposed: 80
Where is the thousand marks thou hadst of me?

DROMIO E.

I have some marks of yours upon my pate,
Some of my mistress' marks upon my shoulders,
But not a thousand marks between you both.

---

63 *post* haste   64 *post* tavern pillar used for chalking up accounts   66 *maw* stomach (usually applied to animals)   75 *Phoenix* i.e. the house and shop of Antipholus of Ephesus (see I, ii, 9n.)   78 *bestowed* deposited   79 *sconce* head   80 *stands on* engages in

If I should pay your worship those again,
Perchance you will not bear them patiently.

ANTIPHOLUS S.
Thy mistress' marks? What mistress, slave, hast thou?

DROMIO E.
Your worship's wife, my mistress at the Phoenix;
She that doth fast till you come home to dinner,
And prays that you will hie you home to dinner.

ANTIPHOLUS S.
What! wilt thou flout me thus unto my face,
Being forbid? There, take you that, sir knave.
[Strikes him.]

DROMIO E.
What mean you, sir? For God's sake, hold your hands!
94 Nay, an you will not, sir, I'll take my heels.
                                    Exit Dromio [of Ephesus].

ANTIPHOLUS S.
Upon my life, by some device or other
96 The villain is o'er-raught of all my money.
97 They say this town is full of cozenage:
As, nimble jugglers that deceive the eye,
Dark-working sorcerers that change the mind,
Soul-killing witches that deform the body,
101 Disguisèd cheaters, prating mountebanks,
102 And many such-like liberties of sin:
If it prove so, I will be gone the sooner.
I'll to the Centaur to go seek this slave;
I greatly fear my money is not safe.   *Exit.*

*

94 *an* if 96 *o'er-raught* overreached, tricked out of 97 *cozenage* cheating
(Menander and St Paul, among other writers, helped establish the tradition
of Ephesus as a city of magic and trickery) 101 *mountebanks* charlatans
(peddling worthless wares) 102 *liberties of sin* licensed offenders (Steevens)
(but the right word may be 'libertines')

Enter Adriana, wife to Antipholus [of Ephesus], with II, i
Luciana, her sister.

ADRIANA
Neither my husband nor the slave returned,
That in such haste I sent to seek his master?
Sure, Luciana, it is two o'clock.

LUCIANA
Perhaps some merchant hath invited him,
And from the mart he's somewhere gone to dinner.
Good sister, let us dine and never fret.
A man is master of his liberty:
Time is their master, and when they see time,
They'll go or come; if so, be patient, sister.

ADRIANA
Why should their liberty than ours be more?

LUCIANA
Because their business still lies out o'door.   11

ADRIANA
Look, when I serve him so, he takes it ill.

LUCIANA
O, know he is the bridle of your will.

ADRIANA
There's none but asses will be bridled so.

LUCIANA
Why, headstrong liberty is lashed with woe.   15
There's nothing situate under heaven's eye   16
But hath his bound, in earth, in sea, in sky.
The beasts, the fishes, and the wingèd fowls,
Are their males' subjects, and at their controls.
Men, more divine, the masters of all these,
Lords of the wide world, and wild wat'ry seas,
Indued with intellectual sense and souls,   22

II, i Before the house of Antipholus of Ephesus 11 *still* always 15 *lashed*
scourged, whipped 16–24 *There's . . . lords* (Luciana here presents the
traditional idea of male supremacy in 'the great chain of being') 22–25
intellectual sense . . . will (the will, in Renaissance psychology, was supposed
to be guided by the reason, or intellectual sense)

Of more pre-eminence than fish and fowls,
Are masters to their females, and their lords :
Then let your will attend on their accords.

ADRIANA
This servitude makes you to keep unwed.

LUCIANA
Not this, but troubles of the marriage-bed.

ADRIANA
But were you wedded, you would bear some sway.

LUCIANA
Ere I learn love, I'll practise to obey.

ADRIANA
30   How if your husband start some other where ?

LUCIANA
Till he come home again, I would forbear.

ADRIANA
Patience unmoved ! No marvel though she pause ;
They can be meek that have no other cause.
A wretched soul, bruised with adversity,
We bid be quiet when we hear it cry.
But were we burd'ned with like weight of pain,
As much or more we should ourselves complain :
So thou, that hast no unkind mate to grieve thee,
39   With urging helpless patience wouldst relieve me ;
40   But if thou live to see like right bereft,
41   This fool-begged patience in thee will be left.

LUCIANA
Well, I will marry one day but to try.
Here comes your man ; now is your husband nigh.
     Enter Dromio of Ephesus.

ADRIANA
Say, is your tardy master now at hand ?

DROMIO E.   Nay, he's at two hands with me, and that my
two ears can witness.

---

30 *start . . . where* i.e. turn to other women   39 *helpless* futile   40 *like right bereft* a similar injustice   41 *This . . . left* you will leave this foolish plea for patience

ADRIANA
Say, didst thou speak with him? Know'st thou his mind?

DROMIO E.
Ay, ay, he told his mind upon mine ear.
Beshrew his hand, I scarce could understand it.

LUCIANA Spake he so doubtfully, thou couldst not feel
his meaning?

DROMIO E. Nay, he struck so plainly, I could too well feel
his blows; and withal so doubtfully, that I could scarce
understand them. 54

ADRIANA
But say, I prithee, is he coming home?
It seems he hath great care to please his wife.

DROMIO E.
Why, mistress, sure my master is horn-mad. 57

ADRIANA
Horn-mad, thou villain!

DROMIO E. I mean not cuckold-mad;
But, sure, he is stark mad.
When I desired him to come home to dinner,
He asked me for a thousand marks in gold.
''Tis dinner time,' quoth I: 'My gold!' quoth he.
'Your meat doth burn,' quoth I: 'My gold!' quoth he.
'Will you come?' quoth I: 'My gold!' quoth he—
'Where is the thousand marks I gave thee, villain?'
'The pig,' quoth I, 'is burned': 'My gold!' quoth he.
'My mistress, sir—,' quoth I: 'Hang up thy mistress!
I know not thy mistress; out on thy mistress!'

LUCIANA Quoth who?

DROMIO E. Quoth my master.
'I know,' quoth he, 'no house, no wife, no mistress.'
So that my errand due unto my tongue, 72
I thank him, I bear home upon my shoulders;
For, in conclusion, he did beat me there.

54 *understand* stand under   57 *horn-mad* acting like an enraged horned
beast (but Adriana catches first the inevitable quibble on the cuckold's
horns)   72 *due . . . tongue* which my tongue should have performed

ADRIANA

Go back again, thou slave, and fetch him home.

DROMIO E.

Go back again, and be new beaten home?
For God's sake send some other messenger.

ADRIANA

Back, slave, or I will break thy pate across.

DROMIO E.

79   And he will bless that cross with other beating:
80   Between you, I shall have a holy head.

ADRIANA

Hence, prating peasant! Fetch thy master home.

DROMIO E.

82   Am I so round with you as you with me,
That like a football you do spurn me thus?
You spurn me hence, and he will spurn me hither:
If I last in this service, you must case me in leather. *[Exit.]*

LUCIANA

86   Fie, how impatience loureth in your face!

ADRIANA

87   His company must do his minions grace,
88   Whilst I at home starve for a merry look.
Hath homely age th' alluring beauty took
From my poor cheek? Then he hath wasted it.
Are my discourses dull? barren my wit?
If voluble and sharp discourse be marred,
Unkindness blunts it more than marble hard.
94   Do their gay vestments his affections bait?
That's not my fault; he's master of my state.
What ruins are in me that can be found
By him not ruined? Then is he the ground
98   Of my defeatures. My decayèd fair

---

79 *he . . . cross* i.e. he will pay further devotion (blows) to the cross made
by the blow on my head   80 *holy* (pun on 'full of holes')   82 *round* plain-
spoken (with pun on usual meaning)   86 *loureth* scowls   87 *minions*
darlings, girl friends   88 *starve* die   94 *his affections bait* tempt him   98
defeatures disfigurements; *decayèd fair* lost beauty

A sunny look of his would soon repair.
But, too unruly deer, he breaks the pale
And feeds from home; poor I am but his stale.   101

LUCIANA
Self-harming jealousy! fie, beat it hence!

ADRIANA
Unfeeling fools can with such wrongs dispense.   103
I know his eye doth homage otherwhere,
Or else what lets it but he would be here?   105
Sister, you know he promised me a chain;
Would that alone, alone he would detain,
So he would keep fair quarter with his bed!   108
I see, the jewel best enamellèd   109
Will lose his beauty; yet the gold bides still   110
That others touch, and often touching will
Wear gold; and no man that hath a name,
By falsehood and corruption doth it shame.
Since that my beauty cannot please his eye,
I'll weep what's left away, and weeping die.

LUCIANA
How many fond fools serve mad jealousy!

Exit [with Adriana].

*

Enter Antipholus [of Syracuse].   II, ii
ANTIPHOLUS S.
The gold I gave to Dromio is laid up
Safe at the Centaur; and the heedful slave
Is wand'red forth, in care to seek me out
By computation and mine host's report.

---

101 *from* away from; *stale* (1) person taken lightly and for granted, (2) harlot
103 *dispense* pardon (offer dispensation for) **105** *lets* prevents **108** *keep
. . . bed* remain faithful in bed **109–13** *I see . . . shame* (possibly corrupt
owing to omitted line or lines; the general idea seems to be that honor, like
gold, is durable only up to a point, and must be guarded against wear by
those who possess it) **110** *his* its
II, ii A street in Ephesus

I could not speak with Dromio since at first
I sent him from the mart. See, here he comes.
    Enter Dromio of Syracuse.
How now, sir! is your merry humor altered?
As you love strokes, so jest with me again.
You know no Centaur? You received no gold?
10   Your mistress sent to have me home to dinner?
My house was at the Phoenix? Wast thou mad,
That thus so madly thou didst answer me?

DROMIO S.

What answer, sir? When spake I such a word?

ANTIPHOLUS S.

Even now, even here, not half an hour since.

DROMIO S.

I did not see you since you sent me hence,
Home to the Centaur, with the gold you gave me.

ANTIPHOLUS S.

Villain, thou didst deny the gold's receipt,
And told'st me of a mistress, and a dinner;
For which, I hope, thou felt'st I was displeased.

DROMIO S.

I am glad to see you in this merry vein.
What means this jest? I pray you, master, tell me.

ANTIPHOLUS S.

22   Yea, dost thou jeer and flout me in the teeth?
Think'st thou I jest? Hold, take thou that, and that.
    Beats Dromio.

DROMIO S.

24   Hold, sir, for God's sake! Now your jest is earnest.
Upon what bargain do you give it me?

ANTIPHOLUS S.

Because that I familiarly sometimes
Do use you for my fool, and chat with you,
Your sauciness will jest upon my love,
29   And make a common of my serious hours.

22 *in the teeth* to my face   **24** *earnest* (1) serious, (2) down payment to secure
a bargain (see l. 25)   **29** *common* public land

When the sun shines let foolish gnats make sport,
But creep in crannies when he hides his beams.
If you will jest with me, know my aspect,   32
And fashion your demeanor to my looks,
Or I will beat this method in your sconce.   34

DROMIO S. Sconce, call you it? So you would leave bat-
tering, I had rather have it a head. An you use these 36
blows long, I must get a sconce for my head and ensconce 37
it too; or else I shall seek my wit in my shoulders. But I 38
pray, sir, why am I beaten?

ANTIPHOLUS S. Dost thou not know?

DROMIO S. Nothing, sir, but that I am beaten.

ANTIPHOLUS S. Shall I tell you why?

DROMIO S. Ay, sir, and wherefore; for they say every
why hath a wherefore.

ANTIPHOLUS S. Why, first – for flouting me; and then,
wherefore – for urging it the second time to me.

DROMIO S.
Was there ever any man thus beaten out of season,
When in the why and the wherefore is neither rime nor
    reason?
Well, sir, I thank you.

ANTIPHOLUS S. Thank me, sir, for what?

DROMIO S. Marry, sir, for this something that you gave
me for nothing.

ANTIPHOLUS S. I'll make you amends next, to give you
nothing for something. But say, sir, is it dinner-time?

DROMIO S. No, sir, I think the meat wants that I have. 55

ANTIPHOLUS S. In good time, sir; what's that?   56

DROMIO S. Basting.

ANTIPHOLUS S. Well, sir, then 'twill be dry.

DROMIO S. If it be, sir, I pray you eat none of it.

ANTIPHOLUS S. Your reason?

---

32 *aspect* look (basically a planet's astrological portent)   34–37 *sconce*
head; fort; helmet   36 *An* if   37 *ensconce* protect militarily   38 *seek . . .
shoulders* have to find my brains in my shoulders   55 *wants . . . have* lacks
what I have   56 *In good time* indeed

DROMIO S. Lest it make you choleric, and purchase me
62 another dry basting.

ANTIPHOLUS S. Well, sir, learn to jest in good time.
There's a time for all things.

DROMIO S. I durst have denied that, before you were so
choleric.

ANTIPHOLUS S. By what rule, sir?

68 DROMIO S. Marry, sir, by a rule as plain as the plain bald
pate of Father Time himself.

ANTIPHOLUS S. Let's hear it.

DROMIO S. There's no time for a man to recover his hair
that grows bald by nature.

73 ANTIPHOLUS S. May he not do it by fine and recovery?

DROMIO S. Yes, to pay a fine for a periwig and recover
the lost hair of another man.

ANTIPHOLUS S. Why is Time such a niggard of hair,
77 being, as it is, so plentiful an excrement?

DROMIO S. Because it is a blessing that he bestows on
beasts; and what he hath scanted men in hair, he hath
given them in wit.

ANTIPHOLUS S. Why, but there's many a man hath more
hair than wit.

DROMIO S. Not a man of those but he hath the wit to lose
his hair.

ANTIPHOLUS S. Why, thou didst conclude hairy men
plain dealers without wit.

87 DROMIO S. The plainer dealer, the sooner lost; yet he
loseth it in a kind of jollity.

ANTIPHOLUS S. For what reason?

90 DROMIO S. For two; and sound ones too.

ANTIPHOLUS S. Nay, not sound, I pray you.

---

62 *dry basting* hard beating (properly, not drawing blood) **68** *Marry* by
the Virgin Mary (grown to be only a mild oath) **73** *fine and recovery*
(quibble on legal procedure for gaining absolute ownership) **77** *excrement*
something, like hair, that grows from the body **87–88** *The . . . jollity*
(alluding to loss of hair from venereal disease) **90–93** *sound ones . . .*
falsing (carrying out the witticism on the loss of hair and the wig)

DROMIO S. Sure ones, then.

ANTIPHOLUS S. Nay, not sure, in a thing falsing.

DROMIO S. Certain ones, then.

ANTIPHOLUS S. Name them.

DROMIO S. The one, to save the money that he spends in
tiring ; the other, that at dinner they should not drop in   97
his porridge.

ANTIPHOLUS S. You would all this time have proved,
there is no time for all things.

DROMIO S. Marry, and did, sir ; namely, no time to
recover hair lost by nature.

ANTIPHOLUS S. But your reason was not substantial,
why there is no time to recover.

DROMIO S. Thus I mend it : Time himself is bald, and
therefore to the world's end will have bald followers.   106

ANTIPHOLUS S. I knew 'twould be a bald conclusion.
But soft ! who wafts us yonder ?
Enter Adriana and Luciana.

ADRIANA
Ay, ay, Antipholus, look strange and frown.   109
Some other mistress hath thy sweet aspects ;   110
I am not Adriana, nor thy wife.
The time was once when thou unurged wouldst vow
That never words were music to thine ear,
That never object pleasing in thine eye,
That never touch well welcome to thy hand,
That never meat sweet-savored in thy taste,
Unless I spake, or looked, or touched, or carved to thee.
How comes it now, my husband, O, how comes it,
That thou art then estrangèd from thyself ?
Thyself I call it, being strange to me,
That, undividable, incorporate,
Am better than thy dear self's better part.
Ah, do not tear away thyself from me !

97 *tiring* dressing (the hair)   106 *bald* paltry, lame (besides the continued
reference to the head)   109 *strange* estranged (cf. ll. 119, 120)   110 *aspects*
countenance (cf. l. 32)

47

124   For know, my love, as easy mayst thou fall
      A drop of water in the breaking gulf,
      And take unmingled thence that drop again
      Without addition or diminishing,
      As take from me thyself and not me too.
      How dearly would it touch thee to the quick,
130   Shouldst thou but hear I were licentious,
      And that this body, consecrate to thee,
      By ruffian lust should be contaminate!
      Wouldst thou not spit at me, and spurn at me,
      And hurl the name of husband in my face,
      And tear the stained skin off my harlot-brow,
      And from my false hand cut the wedding-ring,
      And break it with a deep-divorcing vow?
      I know thou canst, and therefore see thou do it.
      I am possessed with an adulterate blot;
      My blood is mingled with the crime of lust.
      For if we two be one, and thou play false,
      I do digest the poison of thy flesh,
      Being strumpeted by thy contagion.
      Keep then fair league and truce with thy true bed;
145   I live distained, thou undishonorèd.

ANTIPHOLUS S.
      Plead you to me, fair dame? I know you not.
      In Ephesus I am but two hours old,
      As strange unto your town as to your talk;
      Who every word by all my wit being scanned,
      Wants wit in all, one word to understand.

LUCIANA
      Fie, brother! how the world is changed with you!
      When were you wont to use my sister thus?
      She sent for you by Dromio home to dinner.

ANTIPHOLUS S. By Dromio?

DROMIO S. By me?

124 *fall* let fall   145 *distained* unstained (by contagion)

ADRIANA

By thee; and this thou didst return from him,
That he did buffet thee, and in his blows,
Denied my house for his, me for his wife.

ANTIPHOLUS S.

Did you converse, sir, with this gentlewoman?
What is the course and drift of your compact?   160

DROMIO S.

I, sir? I never saw her till this time.

ANTIPHOLUS S.

Villain, thou liest; for even her very words
Didst thou deliver to me on the mart.

DROMIO S.

I never spake with her in all my life.

ANTIPHOLUS S.

How can she thus then call us by our names?
Unless it be by inspiration.

ADRIANA

How ill agrees it with your gravity
To counterfeit thus grossly with your slave,
Abetting him to thwart me in my mood!
Be it my wrong you are from me exempt,   170
But wrong not that wrong with a more contempt.
Come, I will fasten on this sleeve of thine:
Thou art an elm, my husband, I a vine,
Whose weakness married to thy stronger state
Makes me with thy strength to communicate.
If aught possess thee from me, it is dross,   176
Usurping ivy, brier, or idle moss;   177
Who all for want of pruning, with intrusion
Infect thy sap and live on thy confusion.   179

ANTIPHOLUS S.

To me she speaks; she moves me for her theme.   180
What, was I married to her in my dream?

160 *compact* conspiracy   170 *exempt* cut off   176 *possess* take   177 *idle*
worthless   179 *confusion* destruction   180 *moves* appeals to

Or sleep I now, and think I hear all this?
183   What error drives our eyes and ears amiss?
Until I know this sure uncertainty,
185   I'll entertain the offered fallacy.

LUCIANA
Dromio, go bid the servants spread for dinner.

DROMIO S.
187   O, for my beads! I cross me for a sinner.
This is the fairy land. O spite of spites,
We talk with goblins, owls, and sprites!
If we obey them not, this will ensue:
They'll suck our breath, or pinch us black and blue.

LUCIANA
Why prat'st thou to thyself and answer'st not?
Dromio, thou drone, thou snail, thou slug, thou sot!

DROMIO S.
194   I am transformèd, master, am I not?

ANTIPHOLUS S.
I think thou art, in mind, and so am I.

DROMIO S.
Nay, master, both in mind and in my shape.

ANTIPHOLUS S.
Thou hast thine own form.   No, I am an ape.

DROMIO S.

LUCIANA
If thou art changed to aught, 'tis to an ass.

DROMIO S.
'Tis true; she rides me, and I long for grass.
'Tis so, I am an ass; else it could never be
But I should know her as well as she knows me.

ADRIANA
Come, come, no longer will I be a fool,

183 *error* (here, as elsewhere in the play, the word suggests the uncanny illusions of Ephesus; cf. ll. 188–89)   185 *entertain . . . fallacy* accept what seems to be true   187 *beads* rosary   194–98 *I . . . ass* (though influenced by Lyly here, Shakespeare was also in the mood that was to create the 'translated' Bottom of *A Midsummer Night's Dream*)

To put the finger in the eye and weep,
Whilst man and master laughs my woes to scorn.
Come, sir, to dinner. Dromio, keep the gate.
Husband, I'll dine above with you to-day,   206
And shrive you of a thousand idle pranks.   207
Sirrah, if any ask you for your master,   208
Say he dines forth, and let no creature enter.
Come, sister. Dromio, play the porter well.

ANTIPHOLUS S.

Am I in earth, in heaven, or in hell?
Sleeping or waking? mad or well advised?   212
Known unto these, and to myself disguised!
I'll say as they say, and persever so,
And in this mist at all adventures go.

DROMIO S.

Master, shall I be porter at the gate?

ADRIANA

Ay; and let none enter, lest I break your pate.

LUCIANA

Come, come, Antipholus, we dine too late.   *[Exeunt.]*

❋

Enter Antipholus of Ephesus, his man Dromio, Angelo III, i
the Goldsmith, and Balthazar the Merchant.

ANTIPHOLUS E.

Good Signior Angelo, you must excuse us all;
My wife is shrewish when I keep not hours.
Say that I lingered with you at your shop
To see the making of her carcanet,   4
And that to-morrow you will bring it home.

---

206 *dine above* (The dinner would presumably be seen 'above', i.e. on the
upper stage. In Elizabethan homes the living quarters were on an upper
floor, while the place of business was on the ground level.)   **207** *shrive you*
hear your confession   **208** *Sirrah* (term of address for servants and other
social inferiors)   **212** *well advised* sane
III, i Before the house of Antipholus of Ephesus   **4** *carcanet* necklace of
gold, or set with jewels

6   But here's a villain that would face me down
    He met me on the mart, and that I beat him,
    And charged him with a thousand marks in gold,
9   And that I did deny my wife and house.
    Thou drunkard, thou, what didst thou mean by this?

DROMIO E.
    Say what you will, sir, but I know what I know;
12 That you beat me at the mart, I have your hand to show.
    If the skin were parchment and the blows you gave were
        ink,
    Your own handwriting would tell you what I think.

ANTIPHOLUS E.
    I think thou art an ass.

DROMIO E.   Marry, so it doth appear
    By the wrongs I suffer and the blows I bear.
17 I should kick, being kicked; and, being at that pass,
    You would keep from my heels and beware of an ass.

ANTIPHOLUS E.
19 Y'are sad, Signior Balthazar. Pray God, our cheer
20 May answer my good will and your good welcome here.

BALTHAZAR
21 I hold your dainties cheap, sir, and your welcome dear.

ANTIPHOLUS E.
    O, Signior Balthazar, either at flesh or fish,
    A table-full of welcome makes scarce one dainty dish.

BALTHAZAR
24 Good meat, sir, is common; that every churl affords.

ANTIPHOLUS E.
    And welcome more common, for that's nothing but
        words.

BALTHAZAR
    Small cheer and great welcome makes a merry feast.

---

6 *face me down* outface me (with the assertion)   9 *deny* disclaim   12 *hand*
handiwork (on my body. 'Hand' could also mean handwriting.)   17 *at that
pass* in that direction   19 *sad* serious (its usual meaning in Shakespeare);
cheer hospitality   19–29 *Y'are . . . heart* (there is delightful irony in this
exchange of courtesies for a dinner that will not take place)   20 *answer*
correspond to   21 *dainties* delicacies   24 *churl* peasant

ANTIPHOLUS E.

Ay, to a niggardly host and more sparing guest.

But though my cates be mean, take them in good part; 28

Better cheer may you have, but not with better heart.

But soft! my door is locked. Go bid them let us in.

DROMIO E.

Maud, Bridget, Marian, Cicely, Gillian, Ginn!

DROMIO S. [within]

Mome, malt-horse, capon, coxcomb, idiot, patch! 32

Either get thee from the door or sit down at the hatch. 33

Dost thou conjure for wenches, that thou call'st for such 34

store,

When one is one too many? Go get thee from the door.

DROMIO E.

What patch is made our porter? My master stays in the

street.

DROMIO S. [within]

Let him walk from whence he came, lest he catch cold

on's feet.

ANTIPHOLUS E.

Who talks within there? Ho, open the door!

DROMIO S. [within]

Right, sir; I'll tell you when, an you'll tell me wherefore.

ANTIPHOLUS E.

Wherefore? For my dinner: I have not dined to-day.

DROMIO S.

Nor to-day here you must not; come again when you

may.

ANTIPHOLUS E.

What art thou that keep'st me out from the house I owe? 42

DROMIO S. [within]

The porter for this time, sir, and my name is Dromio.

28 *cates* delicacies; *mean* plain   32 *Mome, patch* (both words mean 'fool')
33 *hatch* half door; gate or wicket with an open space above   34 *conjure for*
bring into being by magic; *store* quantity (of wenches)   42 *owe* own
(frequent meaning)

DROMIO E.

O villain, thou hast stol'n both mine office and my name!
45 The one ne'er got me credit, the other mickle blame.
If thou hadst been Dromio to-day in my place,
47 Thou wouldst have changed thy face for a name, or thy
name for an ass.

Enter Luce [within].

LUCE *[within]*
48 What a coil is there, Dromio! Who are those at the gate?

DROMIO E.

Let my master in, Luce.

LUCE *[within]*   Faith, no; he comes too late;
And so tell your master.

DROMIO E.   O Lord, I must laugh!
51 Have at you with a proverb: Shall I set in my staff?

LUCE *[within]*
52 Have at you with another: that's – When? Can you tell?

DROMIO S. *[within]*

If thy name be called Luce – Luce, thou hast answered
him well.

ANTIPHOLUS E.

Do you hear, you minion? You'll let us in, I hope?

LUCE *[within]*

I thought to have asked you.

DROMIO S. *[within]*   And you said no.

DROMIO E.

So come, help: well struck! There was blow for blow.

ANTIPHOLUS E.

Thou baggage, let me in.

LUCE *[within]*   Can you tell for whose sake?

---

45 *mickle* much   47 *Thou . . . ass* (obscure; Dromio E. may mean that the
name brought his face into trouble, so that, with the beatings, an ass would
have been more appropriate)   48 *Who . . . gate* (both Luce and Adriana are
on the upper stage and hence unable to see Antipholus E. and Dromio E.,
who are by the rear door *under* the balcony)   51 *Have . . . proverb* I'll throw a
proverb at you; *set . . . staff* claim my home   52 *When . . . tell* (another
proverb, used to evade a question)

DROMIO E.
Master, knock the door hard.

LUCE [*within*]   Let him knock till it ache.

ANTIPHOLUS E.
You'll cry for this, minion, if I beat the door down.   59

LUCE [*within*]
What needs all that, and a pair of stocks in the town?   60
       Enter Adriana [*within*].

ADRIANA [*within*]
Who is that at the door that keeps all this noise?

DROMIO S. [*within*]
By my troth, your town is troubled with unruly boys.

ANTIPHOLUS E.
Are you there, wife? You might have come before.

ADRIANA [*within*]
Your wife, sir knave! Go get you from the door.

DROMIO E.
If you went in pain, master, this 'knave' would go sore.

ANGELO
Here is neither cheer, sir, nor welcome; we would fain
have either.

BALTHAZAR
In debating which was best, we shall part with neither.

DROMIO E.
They stand at the door, master; bid them welcome
hither.

ANTIPHOLUS E.
There is something in the wind, that we cannot get in.

DROMIO E.
You would say so, master, if your garments were thin.
Your cake here is warm within; you stand here in the
cold.
It would make a man mad as a buck to be so bought and   72
sold.

59 *minion* hussy   **60** *What . . . town* why need we be pestered with these
ruffians when the town has stocks   **72** *mad as a buck* i.e. in mating season;
bought and sold used

ANTIPHOLUS E.
  Go fetch me something; I'll break ope the gate.

DROMIO S. *[within]*
  Break any breaking here, and I'll break your knave's pate.

DROMIO E.
  A man may break a word with you, sir, and words are
      but wind:
  Ay, and break it in your face, so he break it not behind.

DROMIO S. *[within]*
77 It seems thou want'st breaking. Out upon thee, hind!

DROMIO E.
  Here's too much 'Out upon thee!' I pray thee, let me in.

DROMIO S. *[within]*
  Ay, when fowls have no feathers, and fish have no fin.

ANTIPHOLUS E.
80 Well, I'll break in. Go borrow me a crow.

DROMIO E.
  A crow without feather? Master, mean you so?
  For a fish without a fin, there's a fowl without a feather:
83 If a crow help us in, sirrah, we'll pluck a crow together.

ANTIPHOLUS E.
  Go get thee gone; fetch me an iron crow.

BALTHAZAR
  Have patience, sir; O let it not be so!
  Herein you war against your reputation,
87 And draw within the compass of suspect
  Th' unviolated honor of your wife.
89 Once this – your long experience of her wisdom,
  Her sober virtue, years, and modesty,
  Plead on her part some cause to you unknown;
92 And doubt not, sir, but she will well excuse
93 Why at this time the doors are made against you.
  Be ruled by me: depart in patience,
  And let us to the Tiger all to dinner;

77 *hind* servant 80 *crow* crowbar 83 *pluck a crow* pick a bone, settle
accounts 87 *draw . . . suspect* bring under suspicion 89 *Once this* in one
word (?), once you do this (?) 92 *excuse* explain 93 *made* shut

And about evening come yourself alone,
To know the reason of this strange restraint.
If by strong hand you offer to break in   98
Now in the stirring passage of the day,   99
A vulgar comment will be made of it,   100
And that supposèd by the common rout
Against your yet ungallèd estimation,   102
That may with foul intrusion enter in
And dwell upon your grave when you are dead;
For slander lives upon succession,   105
For ever housed where it gets possession.

ANTIPHOLUS E.

You have prevailed: I will depart in quiet,
And in despite of mirth mean to be merry.   108
I know a wench of excellent discourse,
Pretty and witty, wild and yet, too, gentle.
There will we dine. This woman that I mean,
My wife – but, I protest, without desert –   112
Hath oftentimes upbraided me withal:
To her will we to dinner. *[to Angelo]* Get you home
And fetch the chain; by this I know 'tis made.   115
Bring it, I pray you, to the Porpentine;   116
For there's the house. That chain will I bestow,
Be it for nothing but to spite my wife,
Upon mine hostess there. Good sir, make haste.
Since mine own doors refuse to entertain me,
I'll knock elsewhere, to see if they'll disdain me.

ANGELO

I'll meet you at that place some hour hence.

ANTIPHOLUS E.

Do so. This jest shall cost me some expense.   *Exeunt.*

*

98 *offer* try   99 *stirring passage* bustle   100 *vulgar* by *the common rout* (next
line; not usually 'cheap')   102 *yet . . . estimation* hitherto untouched
reputation   105 *slander . . . succession* one slander takes over, as in 'succession,' from the preceding one   108 *in . . . mirth* despite mockery (?),
though lacking mirth (?)   112 *without desert* unjustly   115 *by this* by this
time   116 *Porpentine* Porcupine (here the name of an inn)

III, ii   *Enter Luciana, with Antipholus of Syracuse.*

LUCIANA

And may it be that you have quite forgot
A husband's office ? Shall, Antipholus,
3   Even in the spring of love, thy love-springs rot ?
Shall love, in building, grow so ruinous ?
If you did wed my sister for her wealth,
6   Then for her wealth's sake use her with more kindness :
Or if you like elsewhere, do it by stealth ;
Muffle your false love with some show of blindness :
Let not my sister read it in your eye ;
10   Be not thy tongue thy own shame's orator ;
11   Look sweet, speak fair, become disloyalty ;
12   Apparel vice like virtue's harbinger ;
Bear a fair presence, though your heart be tainted ;
14   Teach sin the carriage of a holy saint ;
Be secret-false : what need she be acquainted ?
16   What simple thief brags of his own attaint ?
'Tis double wrong to truant with your bed,
18   And let her read it in thy looks at board.
19   Shame hath a bastard fame, well managèd ;
Ill deeds is doubled with an evil word.
Alas, poor women ! make us but believe,
22   Being compact of credit, that you love us ;
Though others have the arm, show us the sleeve ;
24   We in your motion turn, and you may move us.
Then, gentle brother, get you in again ;
Comfort my sister, cheer her, call her wife.
27   'Tis holy sport to be a little vain,
When the sweet breath of flattery conquers strife.

III, ii The same   3 *love-springs* love-shoots (as of a plant)   6 *wealth's*
welfare's   10 *orator* advocate   11 *become disloyalty* make disloyalty seem
becoming (attractive)   12 *harbinger* herald, advance messenger to a court
14 *carriage* manners   16 *attaint* disgrace, crime   18 *board* table   19
bastard fame counterfeit reputation   22 *compact of credit* composed of
credulity, i.e. made so that (we) will believe anything   24 *We . . . turn* our
moves are governed by yours   27 *vain* false

ANTIPHOLUS S.

Sweet mistress – what your name is else, I know not,
Nor by what wonder you do hit of mine –   30
Less in your knowledge and your grace you show not
Than our earth's wonder; more than earth divine.   32
Teach me, dear creature, how to think and speak;
Lay open to my earthy-gross conceit,   34
Smothered in errors, feeble, shallow, weak,
The folded meaning of your words' deceit.   36
Against my soul's pure truth why labor you
To make it wander in an unknown field?
Are you a god? Would you create me new?
Transform me then, and to your power I'll yield.
But if that I am I, then well I know
Your weeping sister is no wife of mine,
Nor to her bed no homage do I owe.
Far more, far more, to you do I decline.   44
O train me not, sweet mermaid, with thy note,   45
To drown me in thy sister's flood of tears!
Sing, siren, for thyself, and I will dote.
Spread o'er the silver waves thy golden hairs,
And as a bed I'll take them and there lie;
And in that glorious supposition think
He gains by death that hath such means to die.
Let Love, being light, be drownèd if she sink!   52

LUCIANA

What, are you mad, that you do reason so?

ANTIPHOLUS S.

Not mad, but mated; how, I do not know.   54

LUCIANA

It is a fault that springeth from your eye.

ANTIPHOLUS S.

For gazing on your beams, fair sun, being by.

30 *hit of* hit upon   32 *our earth's wonder* Elizabeth I (?)   34 *earthy-gross
conceit* wit gross as earth   36 *folded* i.e. so as to be concealed   44 *decline*
incline   45 *train* entice; *note* music   52 *light* (1) light in weight, (2)
wanton   54 *mated* (1) amazed, (2) confounded, (3) married

LUCIANA
Gaze where you should, and that will clear your sight.

ANTIPHOLUS S.
58   As good to wink, sweet love, as look on night.

LUCIANA
Why call you me love? Call my sister so.

ANTIPHOLUS S.
Thy sister's sister.

LUCIANA   That's my sister.

ANTIPHOLUS S.   No;
It is thyself, mine own self's better part;
Mine eye's clear eye, my dear heart's dearer heart;
My food, my fortune, and my sweet hope's aim;
64   My sole earth's heaven, and my heaven's claim.

LUCIANA
All this my sister is, or else should be.

ANTIPHOLUS S.
66   Call thyself sister, sweet, for I am thee.
Thee will I love, and with thee lead my life;
Thou hast no husband yet, nor I no wife.
Give me thy hand.

LUCIANA   O, soft, sir! hold you still.
I'll fetch my sister, to get her good will.   *Exit.*
     Enter Dromio of Syracuse.

ANTIPHOLUS S.   Why, how now, Dromio! Where runn'st
thou so fast?

DROMIO S.   Do you know me, sir? Am I Dromio? Am I
your man? Am I myself?

ANTIPHOLUS S.   Thou art Dromio, thou art my man,
thou art thyself.

DROMIO S.   I am an ass, I am a woman's man, and besides
myself.

ANTIPHOLUS S.   What woman's man? and how besides
80   thyself?

---

58 *wink* close the eyes (usual meaning in Shakespeare)   **64** *My ... claim* my
only heaven on earth, and my claim given me by (or to) heaven   **66** *am*
(often emended to 'aim' – unnecessarily, in view of l. 61)

DROMIO S. Marry, sir, besides myself, I am due to a
woman: one that claims me, one that haunts me, one
that will have me.

ANTIPHOLUS S. What claim lays she to thee?

DROMIO S. Marry, sir, such claim as you would lay to
your horse; and she would have me as a beast: not that, 86
I being a beast, she would have me; but that she, being a
very beastly creature, lays claim to me.

ANTIPHOLUS S. What is she?

DROMIO S. A very reverent body; aye, such a one as a
man may not speak of, without he say, 'Sir-reverence.' 91
I have but lean luck in the match, and yet is she a 92
wondrous fat marriage.

ANTIPHOLUS S. How dost thou mean a fat marriage?

DROMIO S. Marry, sir, she's the kitchen-wench, and all
grease; and I know not what use to put her to, but to 96
make a lamp of her, and run from her by her own light.
I warrant, her rags and the tallow in them will burn a
Poland winter. If she lives till doomsday, she'll burn a
week longer than the whole world.

ANTIPHOLUS S. What complexion is she of?

DROMIO S. Swart, like my shoe, but her face nothing like 102
so clean kept: for why? She sweats; a man may go over 103
shoes in the grime of it.

ANTIPHOLUS S. That's a fault that water will mend.

DROMIO S. No, sir, 'tis in grain; Noah's flood could not 106
do it.

ANTIPHOLUS S. What's her name?

DROMIO S. Nell, sir; but her name and three quarters – 109
that's an ell and three-quarters – will not measure her 110

---

86 *a beast* (pun on 'abased,' since 'beast' was pronounced 'baste') 91 *Sir-reverence* if you will pardon the expression (corruption of 'saving reverence')
92 *lean* poor, scanty (besides the obvious contrast with *fat*) 96 *grease*
(another bad pun, 'grease' being pronounced 'grace') 102 *Swart* dark
103 *for why?* (the question mark in the folio text may be unnecessary, since
'for why' meant 'because') 106 *in grain* fast dyed, ingrained 109 *Nell*
(hitherto called Luce) 110 *ell* forty-five inches (Nell *bears some breadth* –
almost seven feet in circumference)

from hip to hip.

ANTIPHOLUS S. Then she bears some breadth?

DROMIO S. No longer from head to foot than from hip to
114   hip: she is spherical, like a globe; I could find out countries in her.

ANTIPHOLUS S. In what part of her body stands Ireland?

DROMIO S. Marry, sir, in her buttocks. I found it out by
the bogs.

ANTIPHOLUS S. Where Scotland?

DROMIO S. I found it by the barrenness; hard in the palm
of the hand.

122 ANTIPHOLUS S. Where France?

DROMIO S. In her forehead, armed and reverted, making
war against her heir.

ANTIPHOLUS S. Where England?

DROMIO S. I looked for the chalky cliffs, but I could find
127   no whiteness in them; but I guess it stood in her chin,
by the salt rheum that ran between France and it.

ANTIPHOLUS S. Where Spain?

DROMIO S. Faith, I saw it not; but I felt it hot in her
breath.

ANTIPHOLUS S. Where America, the Indies?

DROMIO S. O, sir, upon her nose, all o'er embellished
133   with rubies, carbuncles, sapphires, declining their rich
134   aspect to the hot breath of Spain, who sent whole arma-
135   does of carracks to be ballast at her nose.

114–15 *countries in her* (a favorite Elizabethan source of humor, though
perhaps Shakespeare was here indebted to Rabelais, who has Friar John
map out the head and chin of Panurge)   122–24 *France . . . heir* (See
Introduction for the importance of this passage in dating the play. Cowden
Clarke: 'Mistress Nell's brazen forehead seemed to push back her rough
and rebellious hair, as France resisted the claim of the Protestant heir to the
throne.' But there is also a reference to the 'French disease' – syphilis – and
its destruction of hair.)   127 *them* i.e. Nell's teeth   133–34 *declining . . .
aspect* looking downward   134–35 *armadoes of carracks* armadas of great
merchant ships or galleons (a topical allusion, suggesting that the date of the
play was not much later than 1588)   135 *ballast* freighted

ANTIPHOLUS S. Where stood Belgia, the Netherlands? 136

DROMIO S. O, sir! I did not look so low. To conclude,
this drudge, or diviner, laid claim to me; called me 138
Dromio; swore I was assured to her; told me what privy 139
marks I had about me, as the mark of my shoulder, the
mole in my neck, the great wart on my left arm, that I,
amazed, ran from her as a witch.

And I think, if my breast had not been made of faith,
  and my heart of steel,
She had transformed me to a curtal dog, and made me 144
  turn i' the wheel.

ANTIPHOLUS S.
Go hie thee presently post to the road; 145
And if the wind blow any way from shore, 146
I will not harbor in this town to-night.
If any bark put forth, come to the mart,
Where I will walk till thou return to me.
If every one knows us, and we know none,
'Tis time, I think, to trudge, pack, and be gone.

DROMIO S.
As from a bear a man would run for life,
So fly I from her that would be my wife. *Exit*.

ANTIPHOLUS S.
There's none but witches do inhabit here,
And therefore 'tis high time that I were hence.
She that doth call me husband, even my soul
Doth for a wife abhor. But her fair sister,
Possessed with such a gentle sovereign grace,
Of such enchanting presence and discourse,
Hath almost made me traitor to myself. *160*

---

136 *Belgia, the Netherlands* (usually called the Low Countries) 138
diviner witch, with powers of prophecy 139 *assured* betrothed 144 *curtal*
with shortened tail (hence of no value in hunting); *turn i' the wheel* (dogs
were said to be very good at turning the cooking spits) 145 *hie* hurry;
presently at once; *post* in haste; *road* roadstead or harbor 146 *And if* if

But lest myself be guilty to self-wrong,
I'll stop mine ears against the mermaid's song.
   Enter Angelo with the chain.

ANGELO Master Antipholus –

ANTIPHOLUS S. Ay, that's my name.

ANGELO
I know it well, sir ; lo, here is the chain.
I thought to have ta'en you at the Porpentine ;
The chain unfinished made me stay thus long.

ANTIPHOLUS S.
What is your will that I shall do with this ?

ANGELO
What please yourself, sir ; I have made it for you.

ANTIPHOLUS S.

170 Made it for me, sir ! I bespoke it not.

ANGELO
Not once, nor twice, but twenty times you have.
Go home with it and please your wife withal ;
And soon at supper-time I'll visit you,
And then receive my money for the chain.

ANTIPHOLUS S.
I pray you, sir, receive the money now,
For fear you ne'er see chain nor money more.

ANGELO
You are a merry man, sir ; fare you well.   *Exit.*

ANTIPHOLUS S.
What I should think of this, I cannot tell ;

179 But this I think, there's no man is so vain
That would refuse so fair an offered chain.

181 I see a man here needs not live by shifts,
When in the streets he meets such golden gifts.
I'll to the mart, and there for Dromio stay ;

184 If any ship put out, then straight away.   *Exit.*

*

170 *bespoke* ordered 179 *vain* foolish 181 *shifts* tricks 184 *straight* directly

Enter a [second] Merchant, [Angelo, the] Goldsmith,   IV, i
and an Officer.

2. MERCHANT

You know since Pentecost the sum is due,
And since I have not much importuned you;
Nor now I had not, but that I am bound
To Persia, and want guilders for my voyage.
Therefore make present satisfaction,
Or I'll attach you by this officer.   6

ANGELO

Even just the sum that I do owe to you
Is growing to me by Antipholus;   8
And in the instant that I met with you
He had of me a chain. At five o'clock
I shall receive the money for the same.
Pleaseth you walk with me down to his house,
I will discharge my bond, and thank you too.

Enter Antipholus [of] Ephesus [and] Dromio [of
Ephesus] from the Courtesan's.

OFFICER

That labor may you save; see where he comes.

ANTIPHOLUS E.

While I go to the goldsmith's house, go thou
And buy a rope's end; that will I bestow
Among my wife and her confederates,
For locking me out of my doors by day.
But soft! I see the goldsmith. Get thee gone;
Buy thou a rope, and bring it home to me.

DROMIO E.

I buy a thousand pounds a year! I buy a rope!   21

Exit Dromio [of Ephesus].

IV, i A street in Ephesus   6 *attach* arrest (this type of financial dealing
was common in an age lacking checks and ready cash)   8 *growing* accruing
21 *I . . . rope* (a puzzling line; perhaps Dromio thinks of the rope as an
instrument for beating himself – hence his preposterous analogy)

ANTIPHOLUS E.

22   A man is well holp up that trusts to you.
I promisèd your presence and the chain;
But neither chain nor goldsmith came to me.
Belike you thought our love would last too long
If it were chained together, and therefore came not.

ANGELO

Saving your merry humor, here's the note
How much your chain weighs to the utmost carat,

29   The fineness of the gold, and chargeful fashion,
Which doth amount to three odd ducats more
Than I stand debted to this gentleman.
I pray you see him presently discharged,
For he is bound to sea and stays but for it.

ANTIPHOLUS E.

I am not furnished with the present money;
Besides, I have some business in the town.
Good signior, take the stranger to my house,
And with you take the chain, and bid my wife
Disburse the sum on the receipt thereof.
Perchance I will be there as soon as you.

ANGELO

Then you will bring the chain to her yourself?

ANTIPHOLUS E.

No; bear it with you, lest I come not time enough.

ANGELO

Well, sir, I will. Have you the chain about you?

ANTIPHOLUS E.

43   An if I have not, sir, I hope you have,
Or else you may return without your money.

ANGELO

Nay, come, I pray you, sir, give me the chain.
Both wind and tide stays for this gentleman,
And I, to blame, have held him here too long.

22 *holp* helped   29 *chargeful* costly   43 *An if* if

ANTIPHOLUS E.

Good Lord! you use this dalliance to excuse   48
Your breach of promise to the Porpentine.
I should have chid you for not bringing it,
But, like a shrew, you first begin to brawl.

2. MERCHANT

The hour steals on; I pray you, sir, dispatch.

ANGELO

You hear how he importunes me: the chain!

ANTIPHOLUS E.

Why, give it to my wife and fetch your money.

ANGELO

Come, come, you know I gave it you even now.
Either send the chain or send me by some token.   56

ANTIPHOLUS E.

Fie! now you run this humor out of breath.
Come, where's the chain? I pray you, let me see it.

2. MERCHANT

My business cannot brook this dalliance.   59
Good sir, say whe'r you'll answer me or no.
If not, I'll leave him to the officer.

ANTIPHOLUS E.

I answer you! What should I answer you?

ANGELO

The money that you owe me for the chain.

ANTIPHOLUS E.

I owe you none till I receive the chain.

ANGELO

You know I gave it you half an hour since.

ANTIPHOLUS E.

You gave me none; you wrong me much to say so.

ANGELO

You wrong me more, sir, in denying it.
Consider how it stands upon my credit.   68

---

48 *dalliance* idle delay   56 *send . . . token* give me a token (e.g. a ring)
showing my right to it   59 *brook* endure   68 *how . . . credit* how my credit
is involved

2. MERCHANT

Well, officer, arrest him at my suit.

OFFICER

I do; and charge you in the Duke's name to obey me.

ANGELO

This touches me in reputation.
Either consent to pay this sum for me,
Or I attach you by this officer.

ANTIPHOLUS E.

Consent to pay thee that I never had!
Arrest me, foolish fellow, if thou dar'st.

ANGELO

Here is thy fee; arrest him, officer.
I would not spare my brother in this case,
78   If he should scorn me so apparently.

OFFICER

I do arrest you, sir; you hear the suit.

ANTIPHOLUS E.

I do obey thee till I give thee bail.
But, sirrah, you shall buy this sport as dear
As all the metal in your shop will answer.

ANGELO

Sir, sir, I shall have law in Ephesus,
To your notorious shame, I doubt it not.
    Enter Dromio [of] Syracuse from the bay.

DROMIO S.

Master, there's a bark of Epidamnum
That stays but till her owner comes aboard,
87   And then she bears away. Our fraughtage, sir,
I have conveyed aboard, and I have bought
89   The oil, the balsamum, and aqua-vitae.
90   The ship is in her trim; the merry wind
Blows fair from land; they stay for nought at all
But for their owner, master, and yourself.

---

78 *apparently* openly   87 *fraughtage* baggage   89 *balsamum* balm; *aqua-vitae* spirits   90 *in her trim* rigged and ready

ANTIPHOLUS E.

How now, a madman? Why, thou peevish sheep,   93
What ship of Epidamnum stays for me?

DROMIO S.

A ship you sent me to, to hire waftage.   95

ANTIPHOLUS E.

Thou drunken slave, I sent thee for a rope,
And told thee to what purpose, and what end.

DROMIO S.

You sent me for a rope's end as soon.   98
You sent me to the bay, sir, for a bark.

ANTIPHOLUS E.

I will debate this matter at more leisure,
And teach your ears to list me with more heed.
To Adriana, villain, hie thee straight.
Give her this key, and tell her, in the desk
That's covered o'er with Turkish tapestry,
There is a purse of ducats; let her send it.
Tell her I am arrested in the street,
And that shall bail me. Hie thee, slave, be gone!
On, officer, to prison till it come.

Exeunt [all but Dromio of Syracuse].

DROMIO S.

To Adriana – that is where we dined,
Where Dowsabel did claim me for her husband.   110
She is too big, I hope, for me to compass.
Thither I must, although against my will,
For servants must their masters' minds fulfill.   *Exit.*

❋

93–94 *sheep ... ship* (pronounced similarly; a favorite Elizabethan pun)   95
waftage passage by sea   98 *You ... soon* i.e. you just as likely sent me (for a
rope's end) to be hanged   110 *Dowsabel* i.e. Gentle and Beautiful (from
French '*douce et belle*'; nicely ironic for Nell)

IV, ii   *Enter Adriana and Luciana.*

ADRIANA
 Ah, Luciana, did he tempt thee so ?
2 Mightst thou perceive austerely in his eye
 That he did plead in earnest ? yea or no ?
 Looked he or red or pale, or sad or merrily ?
 What observation mad'st thou in this case
6 Of his heart's meteors tilting in his face ?

LUCIANA
 First he denied you had in him no right.

ADRIANA
8 He meant he did me none ; the more my spite.

LUCIANA
 Then swore he that he was a stranger here.

ADRIANA
 And true he swore, though yet forsworn he were.

LUCIANA
 Then pleaded I for you.

ADRIANA   And what said he ?

LUCIANA
 That love I begged for you he begged of me.

ADRIANA
 With what persuasion did he tempt thy love ?

LUCIANA
14 With words that in an honest suit might move.
 First, he did praise my beauty, then my speech.

ADRIANA
16 Didst speak him fair ?

LUCIANA   Have patience, I beseech.

ADRIANA
 I cannot, nor I will not hold me still ;
18 My tongue, though not my heart, shall have his will.
19 He is deformèd, crooked, old and sere,

IV, ii Before the house of Antipholus of Ephesus   **2** *austerely* plainly
6 *meteors tilting* passions warring   **8** *spite* vexation   **14** *honest* virtuous,
honorable   **16** *Didst . . . fair* i.e. did you, in turn, speak engagingly to him
18 *his* its   **19** *sere* dried up

Ill-faced, worse bodied, shapeless everywhere;
Vicious, ungentle, foolish, blunt, unkind,
Stigmatical in making, worse in mind.   22

LUCIANA
Who would be jealous then of such a one?
No evil lost is wailed when it is gone.

ADRIANA
Ah, but I think him better than I say,
And yet would herein others' eyes were worse.
Far from her nest the lapwing cries away;   27
My heart prays for him, though my tongue do curse.
          Enter Dromio of Syracuse.

DROMIO S.
Here, go – the desk, the purse – sweet, now, make haste.

LUCIANA
How hast thou lost thy breath?

DROMIO S.   By running fast.

ADRIANA
Where is thy master, Dromio? Is he well?

DROMIO S.
No, he's in Tartar limbo, worse than hell.   32
A devil in an everlasting garment hath him;   33
One whose hard heart is buttoned up with steel;
A fiend, a fury, pitiless and rough;
A wolf, nay worse, a fellow all in buff;
A back-friend, a shoulder-clapper, one that counter-   37
     mands
The passages of alleys, creeks, and narrow lands;
A hound that runs counter and yet draws dry-foot well: 39

---

22 *Stigmatical in making* deformed in body   27 *Far . . . away* (the lapwing
protects her nest by flying about elsewhere)   32 *Tartar limbo* (limbo
properly is a benign Christian place in Hell for unbaptized infants; 'Tartar'
combines this with a pagan place of punishment)   33 *everlasting garment*
the leather, or buff (cf. l. 36), uniform of an Elizabethan officer of the law
37 *back-friend* the type of 'friend' (police officer) who claps one on the
back or shoulder; *countermands* prohibits   39 *counter* (1) opposite to the
direction of the game in a hunt, (2) the name of a debtors' prison; *draws
dry-foot* hunts by the scent of the foot

40   One that before the judgment carries poor souls to hell.

ADRIANA
Why, man, what is the matter?

DROMIO S.
42   I do not know the matter; he is 'rested on the case.

ADRIANA
What, is he arrested? Tell me at whose suit.

DROMIO S.
I know not at whose suit he is arrested well;
But he's in a suit of buff which 'rested him, that can I tell.

46   Will you send him, mistress, redemption, the money in
          his desk?

ADRIANA
Go fetch it, sister. – This I wonder at,   *Exit Luciana.*
That he, unknown to me, should be in debt.

49   Tell me, was he arrested on a band?

DROMIO S.
Not on a band, but on a stronger thing:
A chain, a chain. Do you not hear it ring?

ADRIANA
What, the chain?

DROMIO S.
No, no, the bell; 'tis time that I were gone.
It was two ere I left him, and now the clock strikes one.

ADRIANA
The hours come back! That did I never hear.

DROMIO S.
56   O yes; if any hour meet a sergeant, 'a turns back for very
          fear.

ADRIANA
As if time were in debt! How fondly dost thou reason!

---

40 *judgment* (1) legal verdict, (2) day of judgment   42 *'rested on the case*
arrested (1) in a lawsuit, (2) on his skin (case for *matter*)   46 *mistress,*
redemption (possibly should be the fourth folio's 'Mistress Redemption.'
Shakespeare was fond of perpetuating morality-play abstractions. This
reading would carry out the idea of 'judgment'; and cf. Dromio's *Mistress*
Satan, IV, iii, 44.)   49 *band* bond   56 *hour* (pun on similarly pronounced
'whore'); *'a* it, she (usually 'he')

DROMIO S.

Time is a very bankrupt, and owes more than he's worth   58
to season.
Nay, he's a thief too : have you not heard men say,
That time comes stealing on by night and day ?
If 'a be in debt and theft, and a sergeant in the way,
Hath he not reason to turn back an hour in a day ?
        Enter Luciana.

ADRIANA

Go, Dromio ; there's the money, bear it straight,
And bring thy master home immediately.
                        [Exit Dromio of Syracuse.]
Come, sister ; I am pressed down with conceit –   65
Conceit, my comfort and my injury.
                        Exit [with Luciana].

*

        Enter Antipholus of Syracuse.   IV, iii
ANTIPHOLUS S.

There's not a man I meet but doth salute me
As if I were their well-acquainted friend ;
And every one doth call me by my name.
Some tender money to me ; some invite me ;
Some other give me thanks for kindnesses ;
Some offer me commodities to buy.
Even now a tailor called me in his shop
And showed me silks that he had bought for me,
And therewithal took measure of my body.
Sure, these are but imaginary wiles,   10
And Lapland sorcerers inhabit here.   11
        Enter Dromio [of] Syracuse.

---

58 *owes . . . season* (some obscure jest is intended: 'season' may have
several meanings, including 'the opportunity' and 'to keep fresh') 65
conceit thought
IV, iii The mart 10 *imaginary wiles* tricks of the imagination 11 *Lapland*
(famous for sorcery)

DROMIO S. Master, here's the gold you sent me for.
13   What, have you got the picture of old Adam new apparelled?

ANTIPHOLUS S.
What gold is this? What Adam dost thou mean?

DROMIO S. Not that Adam that kept the Paradise, but
that Adam that keeps the prison; he that goes in the
16   calf's skin that was killed for the Prodigal; he that came
behind you, sir, like an evil angel, and bid you forsake
your liberty.

ANTIPHOLUS S. I understand thee not.

DROMIO S. No? why, 'tis a plain case: he that went, like
a base-viol, in a case of leather; the man, sir, that when
22   gentlemen are tired gives them a sob, and 'rests them;
he, sir, that takes pity on decayed men and gives them
24   suits of durance; he that sets up his rest to do more ex-
25   ploits with his mace than a morris-pike.

ANTIPHOLUS S. What, thou mean'st an officer?

DROMIO S. Ay, sir, the sergeant of the band; he that
brings any man to answer it that breaks his band; one
that thinks a man always going to bed, and says, 'God
give you good rest!'

ANTIPHOLUS S. Well, sir, there rest in your foolery. Is
there any ship puts forth to-night? May we be gone?

DROMIO S. Why, sir, I brought you word an hour since
34   that the bark Expedition put forth to-night; and then
35   were you hindered by the sergeant to tarry for the hoy

13–14 *What . . . apparelled* (an obscure allusion to the absence of the
sergeant of law; perhaps Dromio is asking if Antipholus has obtained the
sergeant a new role) 16 *calf's skin . . . Prodigal* (allusion to the fatted calf
killed for the Prodigal Son. This tiresome facetiousness about the leather-
clad sergeant persists through *case of leather* l. 21.) 22 *sob* (Hanmer suggested 'bob'; i.e. the sergeant's tap on the shoulder) 24 *suits of durance*
clothes that last long (but Dromio, tireless punner, means also long-lasting
legal suits – then very common – or cases that end in prison); *sets . . . rest*
plays (at 'primero,' a card game) with all he has 25 *mace* official staff of the
sergeant; *morris-pike* Moorish pike 34 *bark* seagoing vessel 35 *hoy* small
coasting vessel

Delay. Here are the angels that you sent for to deliver 36
you.

ANTIPHOLUS S.
The fellow is distract, and so am I;
And here we wander in illusions.
Some blessèd power deliver us from hence!
Enter a Courtesan.

COURTESAN
Well met, well met, Master Antipholus.
I see, sir, you have found the goldsmith now.
Is that the chain you promised me to-day?

ANTIPHOLUS S.
Satan, avoid! I charge thee tempt me not! 43

DROMIO S. Master, is this Mistress Satan? 44

ANTIPHOLUS S. It is the devil.

DROMIO S. Nay, she is worse; she is the devil's dam. And 46
here she comes in the habit of a light wench, and thereof 47
comes that the wenches say, 'God damn me'; that's as
much as to say, 'God make me a light wench.' It is
written, they appear to men like angels of light; light is
an effect of fire, and fire will burn; ergo, light wenches 51
will burn. Come not near her.

COURTESAN
Your man and you are marvellous merry, sir.
Will you go with me? We'll mend our dinner here. 54

DROMIO S. Master, if you do, expect spoon-meat, or 55
bespeak a long spoon.

ANTIPHOLUS S. Why, Dromio?

DROMIO S. Marry, he must have a long spoon that must
eat with the devil.

---

36 *angels* coins worth about 10s. apiece (but there are still theological over-tones) **43** *avoid* be gone **44** *Mistress Satan* (another character in Dromio's miracle or morality play of the kind dealing with man's salvation) **46** *dam* mother **47** *habit* dress **51** *ergo* therefore (concluding a syllogism) **51–52** *light . . . burn* wanton girls will burn (through disease) **54** *mend* finish (i.e. the courtesan will provide 'dessert') **55** *expect spoon-meat* i.e. you will have to use a utensil

ANTIPHOLUS S.

Avoid then, fiend! What tell'st thou me of supping?
Thou art, as you are all, a sorceress.
I conjure thee to leave me and be gone.

COURTESAN

Give me the ring of mine you had at dinner,
Or, for my diamond, the chain you promised,
And I'll be gone, sir, and not trouble you.

DROMIO S.

66   Some devils ask but the parings of one's nail,
A rush, a hair, a drop of blood, a pin,
A nut, a cherry-stone;
But she, more covetous, would have a chain.
Master, be wise; and if you give it her,
The devil will shake her chain and fright us with it.

COURTESAN

I pray you, sir, my ring, or else the chain.
I hope you do not mean to cheat me so?

ANTIPHOLUS S.

Avaunt, thou witch! Come, Dromio, let us go.

DROMIO S.

75   Fly pride, says the peacock: mistress, that you know.
                  Exit [with Antipholus of Syracuse].

COURTESAN

Now, out of doubt, Antipholus is mad,
77   Else would he never so demean himself.
A ring he hath of mine worth forty ducats,
And for the same he promised me a chain;
Both one and other he denies me now.
The reason that I gather he is mad,
82   Besides this present instance of his rage,

66–71 *Some . . . it* (prose in the folio text; hence irregular lines. The meaning through l. 69 is that, though most witches – cf. l. 74 – demand only a few things belonging to a victim, this woman requires a chain.)   **75** *Fly . . . know* i.e. how strange that the courtesan should, like the proud peacock, de-cry pride (perhaps with play on *pride* in the sense of sexual desire in the female)   **77** *demean* behave   **82** *rage* wild manner, madness

Is a mad tale he told to-day at dinner,
Of his own doors being shut against his entrance.
Belike his wife, acquainted with his fits,
On purpose shut the doors against his way.
My way is now to hie home to his house,
And tell his wife that, being lunatic,
He rushed into my house and took perforce   89
My ring away. This course I fittest choose,
For forty ducats is too much to lose.   *[Exit.]*

*

 Enter Antipholus [of] Ephesus, with a Jailer.   IV, iv
ANTIPHOLUS E.
 Fear me not, man; I will not break away.
 I'll give thee, ere I leave thee, so much money,
 To warrant thee, as I am 'rested for.   3
 My wife is in a wayward mood to-day,
 And will not lightly trust the messenger.
 That I should be attached in Ephesus,   6
 I tell you, 'twill sound harshly in her ears.
  Enter Dromio of Ephesus, with a rope's end.
 Here comes my man; I think he brings the money.
 How now, sir; have you that I sent you for?
DROMIO E.
 Here's that, I warrant you, will pay them all.
ANTIPHOLUS E.
 But where's the money?
DROMIO E.
 Why, sir, I gave the money for the rope.
ANTIPHOLUS E.
 Five hundred ducats, villain, for a rope?
DROMIO E.
 I'll serve you, sir, five hundred at the rate.   14

---

89 *perforce* by force
IV, iv A street   3 *To warrant* as security for   6 *attached* arrested   14
I'll...rate I'll get you five hundred at that price (?)

ANTIPHOLUS E.
To what end did I bid thee hie thee home?

DROMIO E. To a rope's end, sir; and to that end am I
returned.

ANTIPHOLUS E.
And to that end, sir, I will welcome you.
[Beats him.]

OFFICER Good sir, be patient.

DROMIO E. Nay, 'tis for me to be patient; I am in
adversity.

20 **OFFICER** Good now, hold thy tongue.

DROMIO E. Nay, rather persuade him to hold his hands.

22 **ANTIPHOLUS E.** Thou whoreson, senseless villain!

DROMIO E. I would I were senseless, sir, that I might not
feel your blows.

25 **ANTIPHOLUS E.** Thou art sensible in nothing but blows,
and so is an ass.

DROMIO E. I am an ass indeed; you may prove it by my
28 long ears. I have served him from the hour of my nativity
to this instant, and have nothing at his hands for my
service but blows. When I am cold, he heats me with
beating; when I am warm, he cools me with beating. I
am waked with it when I sleep, raised with it when I sit,
driven out of doors with it when I go from home, wel-
comed home with it when I return; nay, I bear it on my
35 shoulders, as a beggar wont her brat; and, I think, when
he hath lamed me, I shall beg with it from door to door.
*Enter Adriana, Luciana, Courtesan, and a
Schoolmaster, called Pinch.*

ANTIPHOLUS E. Come, go along; my wife is coming
yonder.

---

20 *Good now* for heaven's sake   22 *whoreson* (a coarse epithet with a variety
of intonations; here used to express outraged impatience)   25 *sensible* (1)
intelligent, (2) sensitive   28 *ears* (pun on 'years'; Dromio is saying that he
is a fool for having served so long)   35 *wont* is accustomed (to bear)

DROMIO E. Mistress, respice finem, respect your end; or 38
    rather, the prophecy like the parrot, 'Beware the rope's
    end.'

ANTIPHOLUS E. Wilt thou still talk?
        Beats Dromio.

COURTESAN
    How say you now? Is not your husband mad?

ADRIANA
    His incivility confirms no less.
    Good Doctor Pinch, you are a conjurer;   44
    Establish him in his true sense again,
    And I will please you what you will demand.   46

LUCIANA
    Alas, how fiery and how sharp he looks!   47

COURTESAN
    Mark how he trembles in his ecstasy!   48

PINCH
    Give me your hand and let me feel your pulse.

ANTIPHOLUS E.
    There is my hand, and let it feel your ear.
        [Strikes him.]

PINCH
    I charge thee, Satan, housed within this man,
    To yield possession to my holy prayers,
    And to thy state of darkness hie thee straight.
    I conjure thee by all the saints in heaven.

ANTIPHOLUS E.
    Peace, doting wizard, peace! I am not mad.

ADRIANA
    O that thou wert not, poor distressèd soul!

38 *respice finem* remember (your) end (a pious proverb sometimes taught to
parrots; with this was associated the punning expression *'respice funem,'*
'remember the rope' – or hangman) 44 *you . . . conjurer* i.e. you can expel
evil spirits (as he tried to do, ll. 51–54) 46 *please . . . demand* pay what you
ask 47 *sharp* on edge 48 *ecstasy* madness

ANTIPHOLUS E.

57   You minion, you, are these your customers?
58   Did this companion with the saffron face
      Revel and feast it at my house to-day,
      Whilst upon me the guilty doors were shut
      And I denied to enter in my house?

ADRIANA

      O husband, God doth know you dined at home;
      Where would you had remained until this time,
      Free from these slanders and this open shame!

ANTIPHOLUS E.

      Dined at home! Thou villain, what sayest thou?

DROMIO E.

      Sir, sooth to say, you did not dine at home.

ANTIPHOLUS E.

      Were not my doors locked up and I shut out?

DROMIO E.

68   Perdy, your doors were locked and you shut out.

ANTIPHOLUS E.

      And did not she herself revile me there?

DROMIO E.

70   Sans fable, she herself reviled you there.

ANTIPHOLUS E.

      Did not her kitchen-maid rail, taunt, and scorn me?

DROMIO E.

72   Certes, she did; the kitchen-vestal scorned you.

ANTIPHOLUS E.

      And did not I in rage depart from thence?

DROMIO E.

      In verity you did; my bones bear witness,
      That since have felt the vigor of his rage.

ADRIANA

76   Is't good to soothe him in these contraries?

---

57 *customers* paying visitors   58 *companion* fellow; *saffron* yellow   68
Perdy by God (*par dieu*)   70 *Sans fable* without lying, 'no fooling'   72
kitchen-vestal (her job, according to Dr Johnson, was like that of the vestal
virgins of ancient Rome, to keep the fire burning)   76 *soothe* humor (cf. l. 78)

PINCH
   It is no shame : the fellow finds his vein,
   And yielding to him, humors well his frenzy.

ANTIPHOLUS E.
   Thou hast suborned the goldsmith to arrest me.   79

ADRIANA
   Alas ! I sent you money to redeem you,
   By Dromio here, who came in haste for it.

DROMIO E.
   Money by me ! Heart and good will you might ;
   But surely, master, not a rag of money.   83

ANTIPHOLUS E.
   Went'st not thou to her for a purse of ducats ?

ADRIANA
   He came to me, and I delivered it.

LUCIANA
   And I am witness with her that she did.

DROMIO E.
   God and the rope-maker bear me witness
   That I was sent for nothing but a rope !

PINCH
   Mistress, both man and master is possessed ;
   I know it by their pale and deadly looks.
   They must be bound and laid in some dark room.   91

ANTIPHOLUS E.
   Say, wherefore didst thou lock me forth to-day ?
   And why dost thou deny the bag of gold ?

ADRIANA
   I did not, gentle husband, lock thee forth.

DROMIO E.
   And, gentle master, I received no gold ;
   But I confess, sir, that we were locked out.

ADRIANA
   Dissembling villain ! thou speak'st false in both.

---

79 *suborned* instigated **83** *rag* (cant term for farthing; also money worn
thin) **91** *bound . . . room* (common treatment for madness)

ANTIPHOLUS E.

Dissembling harlot! thou art false in all,
99   And art confederate with a damnèd pack
To make a loathsome abject scorn of me;
But with these nails I'll pluck out these false eyes
That would behold in me this shameful sport.

Enter three or four, and offer to bind him. He strives.

ADRIANA

O, bind him, bind him! Let him not come near me.

PINCH

More company! The fiend is strong within him.

LUCIANA

Ay me, poor man, how pale and wan he looks!

ANTIPHOLUS E.

What, will you murder me? Thou jailer, thou,
I am thy prisoner; wilt thou suffer them
To make a rescue?

OFFICER   Masters, let him go.
He is my prisoner, and you shall not have him.

PINCH

Go bind this man, for he is frantic too.

[They bind Dromio of Ephesus.]

ADRIANA

What wilt thou do, thou peevish officer?
Hast thou delight to see a wretched man
Do outrage and displeasure to himself?

OFFICER

He is my prisoner; if I let him go,
The debt he owes will be required of me.

ADRIANA

116 I will discharge thee ere I go from thee.
Bear me forthwith unto his creditor,
118 And, knowing how the debt grows, I will pay it.
Good Master Doctor, see him safe conveyed

99 *confederate* allied   116 *discharge* relieve of responsibility   118 *how . . .
grows* the reason for the debt

Home to my house. O most unhappy day!   120

ANTIPHOLUS E.

O most unhappy strumpet!

DROMIO E.

Master, I am here entered in bond for you.

ANTIPHOLUS E.

Out on thee, villain! Wherefore dost thou mad me?   123

DROMIO E. Will you be bound for nothing? Be mad, good master: cry, 'The devil!'

LUCIANA

God help, poor souls, how idly do they talk!   126

ADRIANA

Go bear him hence. Sister, go you with me.
Say now, whose suit is he arrested at?

*Exeunt [Pinch and his company with Antipholus
and Dromio of Ephesus]. Manet Officer
[with] Adriana, Luciana, Courtesan.*

OFFICER

One Angelo, a goldsmith; do you know him?

ADRIANA

I know the man. What is the sum he owes?

OFFICER

Two hundred ducats.

ADRIANA   Say, how grows it due?   131

OFFICER

Due for a chain your husband had of him.

ADRIANA

He did bespeak a chain for me, but had it not.

COURTESAN

When as your husband all in rage to-day
Came to my house, and took away my ring –
The ring I saw upon his finger now –
Straight after did I meet him with a chain.

---

120 *unhappy* unfortunate, disastrous (stronger than modern usage)   **123**
mad madden   **126** *idly* senselessly   **131** *grows* comes

ADRIANA

It may be so, but I did never see it.

Come, jailer, bring me where the goldsmith is;

I long to know the truth hereof at large.

> *Enter Antipholus of Syracuse with his rapier drawn,*
> *and Dromio of Syracuse.*

LUCIANA

God, for thy mercy! They are loose again.

ADRIANA

142   And come with naked swords.

143   Let's call more help to have them bound again.

> *Run all out.*

OFFICER   Away! they'll kill us.

> *Exeunt omnes, as fast as may be, frighted.*

ANTIPHOLUS S.

I see these witches are afraid of swords.

DROMIO S.

She that would be your wife now ran from you.

ANTIPHOLUS S.

Come to the Centaur; fetch our stuff from thence.

I long that we were safe and sound aboard.

DROMIO S.   Faith, stay here this night; they will surely do
us no harm; you saw they speak us fair; give us gold.
Methinks they are such a gentle nation that, but for the
mountain of mad flesh that claims marriage of me, I

153   could find in my heart to stay here still, and turn witch.

ANTIPHOLUS S.

I will not stay to-night for all the town;

Therefore away, to get our stuff aboard.   *Exeunt.*

*

142 *naked* drawn   143–44 (The two stage directions of the folio duplicate
each other. Probably the second was the original direction, and *Run all out*
was written in the margin of the prompt-copy)   153 *still* always

Enter the [Second] Merchant and [Angelo,] the   V, i
    Goldsmith.

ANGELO

  I am sorry, sir, that I have hind'red you ;
  But I protest he had the chain of me,
  Though most dishonestly he doth deny it.

2 . MERCHANT

  How is the man esteemed here in the city ?

ANGELO

  Of very reverend reputation, sir,
  Of credit infinite, highly beloved,
  Second to none that lives here in the city ;
  His word might bear my wealth at any time.   8

2 . MERCHANT

  Speak softly ; yonder, as I think, he walks.   9
      Enter Antipholus and Dromio [of Syracuse] again.

ANGELO

  'Tis so ; and that self chain about his neck
  Which he forswore most monstrously to have.   11
  Good sir, draw near to me, I'll speak to him.
  Signior Antipholus, I wonder much
  That you would put me to this shame and trouble ;
  And not without some scandal to yourself,
  With circumstance and oaths so to deny   16
  This chain which now you wear so openly.
  Beside the charge, the shame, imprisonment,
  You have done wrong to this my honest friend,   19
  Who, but for staying on our controversy,
  Had hoisted sail and put to sea to-day.
  This chain you had of me ; can you deny it ?

ANTIPHOLUS S.

  I think I had ; I never did deny it.

V, i Before a priory   8 *His . . . wealth* he could have had all my wealth on
the strength of his word   9 s.d. *again* (an indication that the action of
'Act V' is continuous with that of 'Act IV')   11 *forswore* denied on oath
16 *circumstance* detailed argument or attempted proof   19 *honest* honorable

2. MERCHANT
Yes, that you did, sir, and forswore it too.

ANTIPHOLUS S.
Who heard me to deny it or forswear it?

2. MERCHANT
These ears of mine, thou know'st, did hear thee.
Fie on thee, wretch! 'Tis pity that thou liv'st
To walk where any honest men resort.

ANTIPHOLUS S.
29   Thou art a villain to impeach me thus:
I'll prove mine honor and mine honesty
31   Against thee presently, if thou dar'st stand.

2. MERCHANT
32   I dare, and do defy thee for a villain.
They draw. Enter Adriana, Luciana, Courtesan,
and others.

ADRIANA
Hold, hurt him not, for God's sake! He is mad.
34   Some get within him, take his sword away.
Bind Dromio too, and bear them to my house.

DROMIO S.
36   Run, master, run; for God's sake, take a house!
This is some priory. In, or we are spoiled.
Exeunt [Antipholus and Dromio of
Syracuse] to the Priory.
Enter Lady Abbess.

ABBESS
Be quiet, people. Wherefore throng you hither?

ADRIANA
To fetch my poor distracted husband hence.
Let us come in, that we may bind him fast,
And bear him home for his recovery.

ANGELO
I knew he was not in his perfect wits.

---

29 *impeach* accuse   31 *presently* at once; *stand* i.e. take your position for
fighting   32 *defy* challenge; *villain* base person   34 *within him* under his
guard   36 *take* i.e. take to

2. MERCHANT
I am sorry now that I did draw on him.

ABBESS
How long hath this possession held the man?

ADRIANA
This week he hath been heavy, sour, sad,
And much different from the man he was;
But till this afternoon his passion
Ne'er brake into extremity of rage.

ABBESS
Hath he not lost much wealth by wrack of sea?
Buried some dear friend? Hath not else his eye
Strayed his affection in unlawful love –   51
A sin prevailing much in youthful men,
Who give their eyes the liberty of gazing?
Which of these sorrows is he subject to?

ADRIANA
To none of these, except it be the last;
Namely, some love that drew him oft from home.

ABBESS
You should for that have reprehended him.

ADRIANA
Why, so I did.

ABBESS   Ay, but not rough enough.

ADRIANA
As roughly as my modesty would let me.

ABBESS
Haply, in private.

ADRIANA   And in assemblies too.

ABBESS
Ay, but not enough.

ADRIANA
It was the copy of our conference.   62
In bed, he slept not for my urging it;   63
At board, he fed not for my urging it;

51 *Strayed* led astray   62 *copy* theme   63 *for* because of

Alone, it was the subject of my theme;
66   In company I often glancèd it.
67   Still did I tell him it was vile and bad.

ABBESS
And thereof came it that the man was mad.
The venom clamors of a jealous woman
Poisons more deadly than a mad dog's tooth.
It seems his sleeps were hind'red by thy railing,
And thereof comes it that his head is light.
Thou say'st his meat was sauced with thy upbraidings;
Unquiet meals make ill digestions;
Thereof the raging fire of fever bred.
And what's a fever but a fit of madness?
Thou sayest his sports were hind'red by thy brawls.
Sweet recreation barred, what doth ensue
But moody and dull melancholy,
Kinsman to grim and comfortless despair,
And at her heels a huge infectious troop
82   Of pale distemperatures and foes to life?
In food, in sport, and life-preserving rest
To be disturbed, would mad or man or beast.
The consequence is, then, thy jealous fits
Hath scared thy husband from the use of wits.

LUCIANA
She never reprehended him but mildly
When he demeaned himself rough, rude, and wildly.
Why bear you these rebukes and answer not?

ADRIANA
90   She did betray me to my own reproof.
Good people, enter, and lay hold on him.

ABBESS
No, not a creature enters in my house.

ADRIANA
Then let your servants bring my husband forth.

---

66 *glancèd* touched upon   67 *Still* always   82 *distemperatures* disorders
90 *She ... reproof* she tricked me into testifying against myself

ABBESS
>   Neither : he took this place for sanctuary,
>   And it shall privilege him from your hands
>   Till I have brought him to his wits again,
>   Or lose my labor in assaying it.

ADRIANA
>   I will attend my husband, be his nurse,
>   Diet his sickness, for it is my office,
>   And will have no attorney but myself ;   100
>   And therefore let me have him home with me.

ABBESS
>   Be patient, for I will not let him stir
>   Till I have used the approvèd means I have,
>   With wholesome syrups, drugs, and holy prayers,
>   To make of him a formal man again.   105
>   It is a branch and parcel of mine oath,   106
>   A charitable duty of my order.
>   Therefore depart and leave him here with me.

ADRIANA
>   I will not hence and leave my husband here ;
>   And ill it doth beseem your holiness
>   To separate the husband and the wife.

ABBESS
>   Be quiet, and depart ; thou shalt not have him.   *[Exit.]*

LUCIANA
>   Complain unto the Duke of this indignity.

ADRIANA
>   Come, go. I will fall prostrate at his feet,
>   And never rise until my tears and prayers
>   Have won his Grace to come in person hither,
>   And take perforce my husband from the Abbess.

2 . MERCHANT
>   By this, I think, the dial points at five :
>   Anon, I'm sure, the Duke himself in person

---

100 *attorney* agent   **105** *formal* in proper form, sane   **106** *branch and parcel* part and parcel

Comes this way to the melancholy vale,
121 The place of death and sorry execution,
Behind the ditches of the abbey here.

ANGELO
Upon what cause?

2. MERCHANT
To see a reverend Syracusian merchant,
Who put unluckily into this bay
Against the laws and statutes of this town,
Beheaded publicly for his offense.

ANGELO
See where they come. We will behold his death.

LUCIANA
Kneel to the Duke before he pass the abbey.

*Enter the Duke of Ephesus, and [Egeon] the
Merchant of Syracuse, bare head, with the Headsman,
and other Officers.*

DUKE
Yet once again proclaim it publicly,
If any friend will pay the sum for him,
132 He shall not die; so much we tender him.

ADRIANA
Justice, most sacred Duke, against the Abbess!

DUKE
She is a virtuous and a reverend lady.
It cannot be that she hath done thee wrong.

ADRIANA
May it please your Grace, Antipholus, my husband,
Who I made lord of me and all I had,
138 At your important letters, this ill day
A most outrageous fit of madness took him,
That desperately he hurried through the street –
With him his bondman, all as mad as he –
Doing displeasure to the citizens

121 *sorry* causing sorrow   132 *tender* grant   138 *important* firmly requesting

By rushing in their houses, bearing thence
Rings, jewels, anything his rage did like.   144
Once did I get him bound and sent him home,
Whilst to take order for the wrongs I went   146
That here and there his fury had committed.
Anon, I wot not by what strong escape,   148
He broke from those that had the guard of him,
And with his mad attendant and himself,
Each one with ireful passion, with drawn swords
Met us again and, madly bent on us,
Chased us away, till, raising of more aid,
We came again to bind them. Then they fled
Into this abbey, whither we pursued them;
And here the Abbess shuts the gates on us,
And will not suffer us to fetch him out,
Nor send him forth that we may bear him hence.
Therefore, most gracious Duke, with thy command
Let him be brought forth and borne hence for help.   160

DUKE

Long since thy husband served me in my wars,
And I to thee engaged a prince's word,
When thou didst make him master of thy bed,
To do him all the grace and good I could.
Go, some of you, knock at the abbey gate
And bid the Lady Abbess come to me.
I will determine this before I stir.
          Enter a Messenger.

MESSENGER

O mistress, mistress, shift and save yourself!
My master and his man are both broke loose,
Beaten the maids a-row and bound the doctor,   170
Whose beard they have singed off with brands of fire;
And ever as it blazed they threw on him
Great pails of puddled mire to quench the hair.

144 *rage* madness   146 *take order* settle   148 *wot* know; *strong* violent
170 *a-row* one by one (or so that they lie in a row)

My master preaches patience to him, and the while
175   His man with scissors nicks him like a fool ;
And sure, unless you send some present help,
Between them they will kill the conjurer.

ADRIANA
Peace, fool ! thy master and his man are here,
And that is false thou dost report to us.

MESSENGER
Mistress, upon my life, I tell you true ;
I have not breathed almost since I did see it.
He cries for you and vows, if he can take you,
To scorch your face and to disfigure you.
        Cry within.
Hark, hark ! I hear him, mistress. Fly, be gone !

DUKE
185   Come, stand by me ; fear nothing. Guard with halberds !

ADRIANA
Ay, me, it is my husband ! Witness you,
That he is borne about invisible.
Even now we housed him in the abbey here,
And now he's there, past thought of human reason.
        Enter Antipholus [of Ephesus] and Dromio of Ephesus.

ANTIPHOLUS E.
Justice, most gracious Duke ! O grant me justice,
Even for the service that long since I did thee,
192   When I bestrid thee in the wars and took
Deep scars to save thy life ; even for the blood
That then I lost for thee, now grant me justice.

EGEON
Unless the fear of death doth make me dote,
I see my son Antipholus and Dromio.

ANTIPHOLUS E.
Justice, sweet Prince, against that woman there !

---

175 *nicks . . . fool* cuts his hair to make him look like an Elizabethan fool
185 *halberds* long spears with a blade   **192** *bestrid thee* stood over and
protected you when you were down

She whom thou gav'st to me to be my wife,
That hath abusèd and dishonored me,
Even in the strength and height of injury!   200
Beyond imagination is the wrong
That she this day hath shameless thrown on me.

DUKE
Discover how, and thou shalt find me just.   203

ANTIPHOLUS E.
This day, great Duke, she shut the doors upon me,
While she with harlots feasted in my house.   205

DUKE
A grievous fault! Say, woman, didst thou so?

ADRIANA
No, my good lord. Myself, he, and my sister
To-day did dine together. So befall my soul
As this is false he burdens me withal!   209

LUCIANA
Ne'er may I look on day, nor sleep on night,
But she tells to your Highness simple truth!

ANGELO
O perjured woman! They are both forsworn;
In this the madman justly chargeth them.

ANTIPHOLUS E.
My liege, I am advisèd what I say,
Neither disturbed with the effect of wine,
Nor heady-rash, provoked with raging ire,
Albeit my wrongs might make one wiser mad.
This woman locked me out this day from dinner.
That goldsmith there, were he not packed with her,   219
Could witness it, for he was with me then;
Who parted with me to go fetch a chain,
Promising to bring it to the Porpentine,
Where Balthazar and I did dine together.

200 in . . . injury to the most injurious extremes   203 Discover reveal   205
harlots vile companions   209 he . . . withal with which he charges me
219 packed in conspiracy

Our dinner done, and he not coming thither,
I went to seek him. In the street I met him,
And in his company that gentleman.
There did this perjured goldsmith swear me down
That I this day of him received the chain,
Which, God he knows, I saw not; for the which
He did arrest me with an officer.

231 I did obey, and sent my peasant home
For certain ducats; he with none returned.

233 Then fairly I bespoke the officer
To go in person with me to my house.
By the way we met

236 My wife, her sister, and a rabble more
Of vile confederates. Along with them
They brought one Pinch, a hungry lean-faced villain,

239 A mere anatomy, a mountebank,
A threadbare juggler, and a fortune-teller,

241 A needy, hollow-eyed, sharp-looking wretch,
A living dead man. This pernicious slave,

243 Forsooth, took on him as a conjurer,
And gazing in mine eyes, feeling my pulse,
And with no face, as 'twere, out-facing me,
Cries out, I was possessed. Then all together
They fell upon me, bound me, bore me thence,
And in a dark and dankish vault at home
There left me and my man, both bound together,
Till, gnawing with my teeth my bonds in sunder,
I gained my freedom, and immediately
Ran hither to your Grace; whom I beseech
To give me ample satisfaction
For these deep shames and great indignities.

ANGELO
My lord, in truth, thus far I witness with him,
That he dined not at home, but was locked out.

231 *peasant* bondman 233 *fairly* politely 236 *rabble* mob 239 *mere*
sheer; *anatomy* skeleton; *mountebank* charlatan, quack 241 *sharp* hungry
243 *took ... as* assumed the role of

DUKE

But had he such a chain of thee, or no?

ANGELO

He had, my lord; and when he ran in here,
These people saw the chain about his neck.

2 . MERCHANT

Besides, I will be sworn these ears of mine   260
Heard you confess you had the chain of him,
After you first forswore it on the mart,
And thereupon I drew my sword on you;
And then you fled into this abbey here,
From whence, I think, you are come by miracle.

ANTIPHOLUS E.

I never came within these abbey walls,
Nor ever didst thou draw thy sword on me.
I never saw the chain, so help me heaven!
And this is false you burden me withal.

DUKE

Why, what an intricate impeach is this!   270
I think you all have drunk of Circe's cup.   271
If here you housed him, here he would have been.
If he were mad, he would not plead so coldly.   273
You say he dined at home; the goldsmith here
Denies that saying. Sirrah, what say you?

DROMIO E.

Sir, he dined with her there, at the Porpentine.

COURTESAN

He did, and from my finger snatched that ring.

ANTIPHOLUS E.

'Tis true, my liege; this ring I had of her.

DUKE

Saw'st thou him enter at the abbey here?

COURTESAN

As sure, my liege, as I do see your Grace.

---

270 *intricate impeach* involved accusation   **271** *Circe's cup* (the enchant-
ress' drink turned men into animals)   **273** *coldly* reasonably

DUKE

Why, this is strange. Go call the Abbess hither.

282 I think you are all mated or stark mad.

Exit one to the Abbess.

EGEON

Most mighty Duke, vouchsafe me speak a word.

Haply I see a friend will save my life,

And pay the sum that may deliver me.

DUKE

Speak freely, Syracusian, what thou wilt.

EGEON

Is not your name, sir, called Antipholus?

And is not that your bondman Dromio?

DROMIO E.

Within this hour I was his bondman, sir;

But he, I thank him, gnawed in two my cords.

Now am I Dromio, and his man, unbound.

EGEON

I am sure you both of you remember me.

DROMIO E.

Ourselves we do remember, sir, by you;

For lately we were bound, as you are now.

295 You are not Pinch's patient, are you, sir?

EGEON

Why look you strange on me? You know me well.

ANTIPHOLUS E.

I never saw you in my life till now.

EGEON

O, grief hath changed me since you saw me last,

299 And careful hours, with Time's deformèd hand,

300 Have written strange defeatures in my face.

But tell me yet, dost thou not know my voice?

ANTIPHOLUS E. Neither.

EGEON Dromio, nor thou?

---

282 *mated* stupefied **295** *Pinch's patient* i.e. bound as Dromio had been while undergoing 'treatment' for madness **299** *careful* full of care **300** *defeatures* worsenings of feature

DROMIO E. No, trust me, sir, not I.

EGEON I am sure thou dost.

DROMIO E. Ay, sir, but I am sure I do not; and whatso-
   ever a man denies, you are now bound to believe him.

EGEON
   Not know my voice! O time's extremity,
   Hast thou so cracked and splitted my poor tongue
   In seven short years, that here my only son
   Knows not my feeble key of untuned cares?   311
   Though now this grainèd face of mine be hid   312
   In sap-consuming winter's drizzled snow,
   And all the conduits of my blood froze up,
   Yet hath my night of life some memory,
   My wasting lamps some fading glimmer left,   316
   My dull deaf ears a little use to hear.
   All these old witnesses – I cannot err –
   Tell me thou art my son Antipholus.

ANTIPHOLUS E.
   I never saw my father in my life.

EGEON
   But seven years since, in Syracusa, boy,
   Thou know'st we parted; but perhaps, my son,
   Thou sham'st to acknowledge me in misery.

ANTIPHOLUS E.
   The Duke and all that know me in the city
   Can witness with me that it is not so.
   I ne'er saw Syracusa in my life.

DUKE
   I tell thee, Syracusian, twenty years
   Have I been patron to Antipholus,
   During which time he ne'er saw Syracusa.
   I see thy age and dangers make thee dote.
        *Enter the Abbess, with Antipholus of Syracuse and
        Dromio of Syracuse.*

311 *my . . . cares* my voice made feeble by discordant cares (the image is the
favorite Elizabethan one of life losing its harmony)   312 *grainèd* furrowed
316 *wasting lamps* dimming eyes

97

ABBESS

    Most mighty Duke, behold a man much wronged.
        All gather to see them.

ADRIANA

    I see two husbands, or mine eyes deceive me!

DUKE

333   One of these men is genius to the other;
    And so of these, which is the natural man,
    And which the spirit? Who deciphers them?

DROMIO S.

    I, sir, am Dromio; command him away.

DROMIO E.

    I, sir, am Dromio; pray let me stay.

ANTIPHOLUS S.

    Egeon art thou not? or else his ghost?

DROMIO S.

    O, my old master! Who hath bound him here?

ABBESS

    Whoever bound him, I will loose his bonds,
    And gain a husband by his liberty.
    Speak, old Egeon, if thou be'st the man
    That hadst a wife once called Emilia,
344   That bore thee at a burden two fair sons.
    O, if thou be'st the same Egeon, speak,
    And speak unto the same Emilia!

EGEON

    If I dream not, thou art Emilia.
    If thou art she, tell me where is that son
    That floated with thee on the fatal raft?

ABBESS

    By men of Epidamnum he and I
    And the twin Dromio all were taken up;
    But by and by rude fishermen of Corinth
    By force took Dromio and my son from them,

333 *genius* attendant spirit (cf. *Julius Caesar*, II, i, 66)   344 *burden* birth

And me they left with those of Epidamnum.
What then became of them, I cannot tell;
I to this fortune that you see me in.

DUKE

Why, here begins his morning story right: 357
These two Antipholuses, these two so like,   358
And these two Dromios, one in semblance –   359
Besides her urging of her wreck at sea –   360
These are the parents to these children,
Which accidentally are met together.
Antipholus, thou cam'st from Corinth first?

ANTIPHOLUS S.

No, sir, not I; I came from Syracuse.

DUKE

Stay, stand apart; I know not which is which.

ANTIPHOLUS E.

I came from Corinth, my most gracious lord –

DROMIO E.

And I with him.

ANTIPHOLUS E.

Brought to this town by that most famous warrior,
Duke Menaphon, your most renownèd uncle.

ADRIANA

Which of you two did dine with me to-day?   370

ANTIPHOLUS S.

I, gentle mistress.

ADRIANA

And are not you my husband?

ANTIPHOLUS E.

No; I say nay to that.

ANTIPHOLUS S.

And so do I; yet did she call me so;

357–62 (in the folio these lines follow l. 346; the present arrangement – almost an inevitable one – is that of the Globe edition, following Capell) **358** *Antipholuses* (four syllables, the 'o' being scarcely heard) **359** *semblance* seeming, appearance **360** *urging* report

And this fair gentlewoman, her sister here,
Did call me brother. *[to Luciana]* What I told you then,
I hope I shall have leisure to make good,
If this be not a dream I see and hear.

ANGELO
That is the chain, sir, which you had of me.

ANTIPHOLUS S.
380   I think it be, sir; I deny it not.

ANTIPHOLUS E.
And you, sir, for this chain arrested me.

ANGELO
I think I did, sir; I deny it not.

ADRIANA
I sent you money, sir, to be your bail,
By Dromio; but I think he brought it not.

DROMIO E.
No, none by me.

ANTIPHOLUS S.
This purse of ducats I received from you,
And Dromio, my man, did bring them me.
I see we still did meet each other's man,
And I was ta'en for him, and he for me,
390   And thereupon these errors are arose.

ANTIPHOLUS E.
These ducats pawn I for my father here.

DUKE
It shall not need; thy father hath his life.

COURTESAN
Sir, I must have that diamond from you.

ANTIPHOLUS E.
There, take it; and much thanks for my good cheer.

ABBESS
Renownèd Duke, vouchsafe to take the pains
To go with us into the abbey here,
And hear at large discoursèd all our fortunes;
And all that are assembled in this place,

That by this sympathizèd one day's error   399
Have suffered wrong, go keep us company,
And we shall make full satisfaction.
Thirty-three years have I but gone in travail   402
Of you, my sons; and till this present hour
My heavy burden ne'er deliverèd.
The Duke, my husband, and my children both,
And you the calendars of their nativity,   406
Go to a gossips' feast, and go with me;   407
After so long grief such Nativity!   408

DUKE
With all my heart I'll gossip at this feast.   409
   Exeunt [all but] the two Dromios and two Brothers.

DROMIO S.
Master, shall I fetch your stuff from shipboard?

ANTIPHOLUS E.
Dromio, what stuff of mine hast thou embarked?

DROMIO S.
Your goods that lay at host, sir, in the Centaur.   412

ANTIPHOLUS S.
He speaks to me. I am your master, Dromio.
Come, go with us; we'll look to that anon.
Embrace thy brother there; rejoice with him.
       Exit [with his Brother].

DROMIO S.
There is a fat friend at your master's house,
That kitchened me for you to-day at dinner;   417
She now shall be my sister, not my wife.

399 *sympathizèd* felt together   402 *in travail* i.e. as in giving birth   406 *you . . . nativity* i.e. the Dromios   407 *Go . . ., and go with me* (the repetition of 'go' is effective if 'me' is stressed); *gossips' feast* christening feast, at which a 'gossip' or godparent, is a sponsor   408 *Nativity* (as repeated and capitalized the word seems to carry the larger significance of a religious festivity)   409 *gossip at* take part in   412 *at host* in charge of the host   417 *kitchened* entertained in the kitchen (but the word is still too good to sacrifice to a paraphrase)

DROMIO E.
    Methinks you are my glass, and not my brother.
    I see by you I am a sweet-faced youth.
    Will you walk in to see their gossiping?

DROMIO S. Not I, sir; you are my elder.

DROMIO E. That's a question; how shall we try it?

DROMIO S. We'll draw cuts for the senior; till then lead thou first.

DROMIO E. Nay, then, thus:
    We came into the world like brother and brother;
    And now let's go hand in hand, not one before another.

                          Exeunt.

A selection of books published by Penguin is listed on the following pages.

For a complete list of books available from Penguin in the United States, write to Dept. DG, Penguin Books, 299 Murray Hill Parkway, East Rutherford, New Jersey 07073.

For a complete list of books available from Penguin in Canada, write to Penguin Books Canada Limited, 2801 John Street, Markham, Ontario L3R 1B4.

The Complete Pelican
SHAKESPEARE

To fill the need for a convenient and authoritative one-volume edition, the thirty-eight books in the Pelican series have been brought together.

THE COMPLETE PELICAN SHAKESPEARE includes all the material contained in the separate volumes, together with a 50,000-word General Introduction and full bibliographies. It contains the first nineteen pages of the First Folio in reduced facsimile, five new drawings, and illustrated endpapers. 9¾ × 7³⁄₁₆ inches, 1520 pages.

SHAKESPEARE

Anthony Burgess

Bare entries in parish registers, a document or two, and a few legends and contemporary references make up the known life of William Shakespeare. Anthony Burgess has clothed these attractively with an extensive knowledge of Elizabethan and Jacobean England for this elaborately illustrated biography. The characters of the men Shakespeare knew, the influence of his life on his plays, and the stirring events that must have been in the minds of author, actors, and audience are engagingly described here by a writer who sees "Will" not as an ethereal bard but as a sensitive, sensual, and shrewd man from the provinces who turned his art to fortune in the most exciting years of England's history. "It was a touch of near genius to choose Mr. Burgess to write the text for a richly illustrated life of Shakespeare, for his wonderfully well-stocked mind and essentially wayward spirit are just right for summoning up an apparition of the bard which is more convincing than most"—David Holloway, *London Daily Telegraph*. With 48 plates in color and nearly 100 black-and-white illustrations.

THE METAPHYSICAL POETS

Edited by Helen Gardner

Over half the poems chosen are from the great metaphysical poets, John Donne, George Herbert, Richard Crashaw, Henry Vaughan, and Andrew Marvell; but outside these the selection aims at presenting a wide range of poets who in varying ways show the influence of Donne and have written poems that merit the title "metaphysical," from Sir Walter Raleigh to John Norris of Bemerton. In the Introduction an attempt is made, not to define "a metaphysical poem," but to describe some of the qualities that distinguish certain poets and poems in this period and make it necessary for us to regard them as forming to some degree a "school of Donne," or what Samuel Johnson called "a race of metaphysical poets." Short biographical notes are provided, and standard editions and biographies are noted. Notes explain any difficult words or unfamiliar ideas. The poems are edited from the original editions, and the source of the text is given. The editor has tried to bear in mind the needs of the general reader, to whom some of the common ideas of the seventeenth century are strange, and also those of the student, who needs a reliable text and to be referred to books in which further information can be found.

Also:

WILLIAM BLAKE: THE COMPLETE POEMS
Edited by Alicia Ostriker

JOHN DONNE: THE COMPLETE ENGLISH POEMS
Edited by A. J. Smith

ANDREW MARVELL: THE COMPLETE POEMS
Edited by Elizabeth Donno

EDMUND SPENSER: THE FAERIE QUEENE
Edited by Thomas P. Roche, Jr.,
with the assistance of C. Patrick O'Donnell, Jr.

THE COMPLETE PLAYS

Christopher Marlowe
Edited by J. B. Steane

In recent years there has been a widening of opinion about Christopher Marlowe; at one extreme he is considered an atheist rebel and at the other, a Christian traditionalist. There is as much divergence in Marlowe's seven plays, and, as J. B. Steane says in his Introduction, that a man's work should encompass the extremes of *Tamburlaine* and *Edward the Second* is one of the most absorbingly interesting facts of literature. The range of Marlowe's small body of work covers such amazingly unlike pieces as *Doctor Faustus* and *The Jew of Malta*. Controlled and purposeful, these plays contain a poetry that enchants and lodges in the mind.

THREE PLAYS
THE WHITE DEVIL, THE DUCHESS OF MALFI, THE DEVIL'S LAW-CASE

John Webster
Introduction and Notes by David C. Gunby

In calling John Webster the "Tussaud Laureate" Bernard Shaw spoke for all the critics who have complained of the atmosphere of charnel house and torture chamber in Webster's plays. Certainly he can be morbid, macabre, and melodramatic, and he exploits to the full the theatrical possibilities of cruelty and violent death. Critics have too often identified Webster's views with those of his characters, however, and neglected his superb poetry and excellent craftsmanship. Though he was writing at a time of social confusion and pessimism, it is possible to see his own universe as an essentially moral one and his vision as deeply religious. On the evidence of the three plays in this volume, Webster can surely be regarded as a great poet and second only to Shakespeare as an English tragedian.

PENGUIN CLASSICS

The Penguin Classics, the earliest and most varied series of world masterpieces to be published in paperback, began in 1946 with E. V. Rieu's now famous translation of *The Odyssey*. Since then the series has commanded the unqualified respect of scholars and teachers throughout the English-speaking world. It now includes more than three hundred volumes, and the number increases yearly. In them, the great writings of all ages and civilizations are rendered into vivid, living English that captures both the spirit and the content of the original. Each volume begins with an introductory essay, and most contain notes, maps, glossaries, or other material to assist the reader in appreciating the work fully. Some volumes available include:

THE PENGUIN ENGLISH LIBRARY

The Penguin English Library Series reproduces, in convenient but authoritative editions, many of the greatest classics in English literature from Elizabethan times through the nineteenth century. Each volume is introduced by a critical essay, enhancing the understanding and enjoyment of the work for the student and general reader alike. A few selections from the list of more than one hundred titles follow:

THE VIKING PORTABLE LIBRARY

In single volumes, The Viking Portable Library has gathered the very best work of individual authors or works of a period of literary history, writings that otherwise are scattered in a number of separate books. These are not condensed versions, but rather selected masterworks assembled and introduced with critical essays by distinguished authorities. Over fifty volumes of The Viking Portable Library are now in print in paperback, making the cream of ancient and modern Western writing available to bring pleasure and instruction to the student and the general reader. An assortment of subjects follows:

SAUL BELLOW   WILLIAM BLAKE

CERVANTES   GEOFFREY CHAUCER

SAMUEL COLERIDGE   JOSEPH CONRAD

DANTE   RALPH WALDO EMERSON

WILLIAM FAULKNER   GREEK READER

THOMAS HARDY   NATHANIEL HAWTHORNE

HENRY JAMES   JAMES JOYCE

D. H. LAWRENCE   HERMAN MELVILLE

JOHN MILTON   FRANÇOIS RABELAIS

POETS OF THE ENGLISH LANGUAGE

MEDIEVAL AND RENAISSANCE POETS: LANGLAND TO SPENSER
ELIZABETHAN AND JACOBEAN POETS: MARLOWE TO MARVELL
RESTORATION AND AUGUSTAN POETS: MILTON TO GOLDSMITH
ROMANTIC POETS: BLAKE TO POE
VICTORIAN AND EDWARDIAN POETS: TENNYSON TO YEATS

ROMAN READER   JOHN STEINBECK

HENRY THOREAU   THORSTEIN VEBLEN

WALT WHITMAN   OSCAR WILDE

PLAYS

IVANOV, THE SEAGULL, UNCLE VANIA, THREE SISTERS,
THE CHERRY ORCHARD, THE BEAR, THE PROPOSAL, A JUBILEE

Anton Chekhov
Translated with an Introduction by Elisaveta Fen

One of a generation on the brink of a tremendous social
upheaval, Anton Chekhov (1860–1904), despite his
flashes of humor, paints in his plays an essentially tragic
picture of Russian society. The plays in this volume,
which include three one-act "jests," all display Chekhov's
overwhelming sense of the tedium and futility of every-
day life. Yet his representation of human relationships
is infinitely sympathetic, and each play contains at least
one character who expresses Chekhov's hope for a brighter
future.

THREE PLAYS
THE FATHER, MISS JULIA, EASTER

August Strindberg
Translated with an Introduction by Peter Watts

August Strindberg (1849–1912) is the most outstanding
playwright in Swedish literature, and this selection includes his three best-known plays. His "realistic" plays
challenged the theatrical traditions of the day and were
largely inspired by his own turbulent life. Both *The
Father* and *Miss Julia,* with their emphasis on the war of
the sexes, were written during the breakup of Strindberg's
first marriage. *Easter* came thirteen years later and is the
most optimistic and serene of the three. His observation
of human nature, especially the behavior of women, is
powerful and ruthless.

THE MISER AND OTHER PLAYS

Molière
Translated with an Introduction by John Wood

Molière (1622–1673) during his lifetime lifted comedy, previously confined to farce, to the pitch of great art and set standards by which in the Western world it has been judged ever since. Today his plays remain for us sparklingly shrewd commentaries on human life. Of the plays in this volume, three—*The Miser, The Would-Be Gentleman,* and *Don Juan*—are major works. *That Scoundrel Scapin* and *Love's the Best Doctor* are examples of Molière's delight in pure entertainment.

THE MISANTHROPE AND OTHER PLAYS

Molière
Translated with an Introduction by John Wood

The Misanthrope is the acknowledged masterpiece of Molière. The portrait of a man doomed to a social wilderness because he cannot concede to convention or compromise his principles, it is comedy elevated to a tragic plane. With it in this volume are two works of almost equal reputation, *Tartuffe* and *The Imaginary Invalid*, together with *A Doctor in Spite of Himself*—one of the best-known farces—and the comedy ballet *The Sicilian*.

FOUR ENGLISH COMEDIES

Edited by J. M. Morrell

The aim of this volume is to provide a selection of English comedies that are established in their own right as classics possessing sufficient universality to appeal to a modern audience but which are not particularly accessible in other editions. For this purpose Ben Jonson (*Volpone*), who apart from Shakespeare was preeminent in the early seventeenth century, chooses himself, and William Congreve (*The Way of the World*) can alone represent the wit and elegance of Restoration comedy. Hardly less inevitable is the choice of Oliver Goldsmith (*She Stoops to Conquer*) and the talented Richard Brinsley Sheridan (*The School for Scandal*) as examples of the rumbustious comedy of the eighteenth century.

D. H. LAWRENCE

NOVELS AND SHORT STORIES

AARON'S ROD

THE COMPLETE SHORT STORIES OF D. H. LAWRENCE
(3 volumes)

FOUR SHORT NOVELS
(LOVE AMONG THE HAYSTACKS, THE LADYBIRD,
THE FOX, THE CAPTAIN'S DOLL)

JOHN THOMAS AND LADY JANE:
THE HITHERTO UNPUBLISHED SECOND VERSION
OF *LADY CHATTERLEY'S LOVER*

KANGAROO

THE LOST GIRL

THE PORTABLE D. H. LAWRENCE
(eight novelettes and stories plus sections of
THE RAINBOW and WOMEN IN LOVE,
poetry, travel, letters, and essays)
Edited and with an Introduction by Diana Trilling

THE RAINBOW

SONS AND LOVERS

SONS AND LOVERS (Viking Critical Library Edition)

WOMEN IN LOVE

OTHER WORKS

APOCALYPSE

THE COMPLETE POEMS OF D. H. LAWRENCE
Edited by Vivian de Sola Pinto and Warren Roberts

PHOENIX:
THE POSTHUMOUS PAPERS OF D. H. LAWRENCE, 1936

PHOENIX II:
UNCOLLECTED, UNPUBLISHED, AND
OTHER PROSE WORKS

PSYCHOANALYSIS AND THE UNCONSCIOUS
and FANTASIA OF THE UNCONSCIOUS

SELECTED LETTERS
Edited by Richard Aldington

W. SOMERSET MAUGHAM

CAKES AND ALE

In this malicious satire on writers the chief characters are a barmaid of the heart-of-gold variety and several eminent men of letters, two of whom may be Thomas Hardy and Hugh Walpole (though W. Somerset Maugham denied it).

THE MOON AND SIXPENCE

A London stockbroker abandons family and career to become a painter, first in Paris and then in Tahiti. Suggested by the life of Paul Gauguin, this powerful novel is a daring exploration of the mentality of a genius.

THE NARROW CORNER

Money, sex, and murder in the East Indies are the ingredients of this thriller, which is also an acid comment on the futility of idealism.

Also:

ASHENDEN
CHRISTMAS HOLIDAY
COLLECTED SHORT STORIES, Volume 1
COLLECTED SHORT STORIES, Volume 2
COLLECTED SHORT STORIES, Volume 4
LIZA OF LAMBETH
THE MAGICIAN
THE MERRY-GO-ROUND
MRS. CRADDOCK
OF HUMAN BONDAGE
THE PAINTED VEIL
THE RAZOR'S EDGE
THE SUMMING UP
UP AT THE VILLA

OTHER CHOICE TITLES FROM PENGUIN

Arthur Miller

AFTER THE FALL

THE CRUCIBLE

Viking Critical Library Edition
THE CRUCIBLE
Text and Criticism
Edited by Gerald Weales

DEATH OF A SALESMAN

Viking Critical Library Edition
DEATH OF A SALESMAN
Text and Criticism
Edited by Gerald Weales

THE PORTABLE ARTHUR MILLER
(DEATH OF A SALESMAN, THE CRUCIBLE,
selections from THE MISFITS, essays, poetry)
Edited by Harold Clurman

A VIEW FROM THE BRIDGE

James Joyce

DUBLINERS

EXILES

FINNEGANS WAKE

A PORTRAIT OF THE ARTIST AS A YOUNG MAN

PLAYS BY BERNARD SHAW

ANDROCLES AND THE LION

THE APPLE CART

ARMS AND THE MAN

BACK TO METHUSELAH

CAESAR AND CLEOPATRA

CANDIDA

THE DEVIL'S DISCIPLE

THE DOCTOR'S DILEMMA

HEARTBREAK HOUSE

MAJOR BARBARA

MAN AND SUPERMAN

THE MILLIONAIRESS

PLAYS UNPLEASANT
(WIDOWERS' HOUSES, THE PHILANDERER,
MRS WARREN'S PROFESSION)

PYGMALION

SAINT JOAN

SELECTED ONE ACT PLAYS
(THE SHEWING-UP OF BLANCO POSNET,
HOW HE LIED TO HER HUSBAND, O'FLAHERTY V.C.,
THE INCA OF PERUSALEM, ANNAJANSKA, VILLAGE WOOING,
THE DARK LADY OF THE SONNETS, OVERRULED,
GREAT CATHERINE, AUGUSTUS DOES HIS BIT,
THE SIX OF CALAIS)